Love in Exile

Brothers in Arms

Samantha KANE

ELLORA'S CAVE
ROMANTICA PUBLISHING

An Ellora's Cave Romantica Publication

www.ellorascave.com

Love in Exile

ISBN 9781419960536
ALL RIGHTS RESERVED
Love in Exile Copyright © 2009 Samantha Kane
Edited by Raelene Gorlinsky.
Cover art by Syneca.

This book printed in the U.S.A. by Jasmine-Jade Enterprises, LLC.

Electronic book publication December 2009
Trade paperback publication December 2009

LOVE IN EXILE

Dedication

∞

For my husband, my family and my readers, who have all been so very patient.

Acknowledgements

∞

This book would not have been completed without the invaluable help of our summer nanny, Amy. We all love and miss her, but wish her well in her new teaching job. I'd also like to thank the General Research Desk librarians at The High Point Public Library, who were able to find all the sources I requested.

Author's Note

A quick nod to the two main sources of information I used for this book. *Cook: The Extraordinary Voyages of Captain James Cook* by Nicholas Thomas (New York, NY: Walker Publishing Company, Inc., 2003) and *Farther Than Any Man: the Rise and Fall of Captain James Cook* by Martin Dugard (New York, NY: Pocket Books, 2001). Both books contained extensive excerpts from Cook's own journals, written during his voyages, and the journals of his officers, crew and fellow scholars.

I used traditional Maori tattoo designs as the inspiration for my description of the hero's *tatau*. Gregory Anderson's mother was from the Friendly Islands, modern-day Tonga, but traditional Tongan designs are lost to history. When Christian missionaries converted the inhabitants of the Friendly Islands in the eighteenth century, the new Christians gave up their *tatatau*, and very few descriptions survived. The *moko* of the Maori, however, were well-documented, and are still popular today. And I confess, I love traditional Maori designs. So the decision to use them was partly based on research, but mostly on my own preferences. I hope readers will indulge me.

Chapter One

&

"Ah, I see the native has returned."

Gregory Anderson turned toward the drawling voice, the other man's malice barely contained beneath his bored, slightly amused tone. It was Hardington. Gregory's first foray into polite society since returning to England and he had to run into one of his least tolerable acquaintances. He hadn't seen Hardington since just after the war. Gregory had spurned his advances, and his offer to invest in Gregory's first voyage. The man was completely untrustworthy.

Gregory raised a brow coolly as he met Hardington's stare and then insolently ran his gaze down the other man's form. Hardington was tricked out beautifully, of course. The man knew the only likeable thing about him was his looks. He was tall, dark, brooding, well built. Too bad his mind was a cesspool.

"You are still astoundingly unappealing, Hardington," Gregory responded politely, "and the answer is still no."

There were gasps from several people standing near and unabashedly eavesdropping. Hardington's face went rigid with dislike as his cheeks turned red. Gregory sighed inwardly. As if his appearance wasn't fodder enough for the gossips, he had lost control of his unruly tongue again. But since they were going to be talking about him over tea tomorrow anyway, he might as well make sure the gossip was as spectacular as he could possibly make it.

Hardington stepped closer. "You are in my world now, Anderson," he ground out quietly. "I would be very careful if I were you."

Gregory looked away from Hardington, disgusted with himself almost as much as the other man. Then he caught sight of Daniel Steinberg smiling at him broadly from the other side of the ballroom and he forgot completely about Hardington's presence.

"Excuse me," Gregory said to no one in particular and moved across the room toward Daniel. It was like swimming against the tide. The brightly colored gowns and waistcoats in the ballroom shone in the candlelight reminding Gregory of the brightly colored fish of the South Seas. And like startled fish, people darted out of his way as he passed.

He knew he was imposing at well over six feet tall, with shoulders so broad his tailor despaired. But he also knew it wasn't his physical presence that made the people around him nervous. It was fear. He was, after all, half savage, and God knew he could revert to his base nature at any moment. He scoffed as two colorless debutantes scuttled out of his way. They need have no fear. He had no desire to throw them down and plunder their inviolate innocence. They appealed to him about as much as Hardington.

Daniel fought through the crowd and met him halfway. "Gregory," he cried in obvious delight. "When did you arrive in town?" He stuck his hand out and grasped Gregory's in a firm handshake as he reached up and squeezed Gregory's shoulder with the other.

Daniel's greeting was so warm that Gregory forgot the cold welcome he'd received so far. "Only yesterday," Gregory replied shaking Daniel's hand with both of his. "God, Daniel, it's good to see you." He knew his smile was as broad as Daniel's. He had missed his old childhood friend these many years he'd been gone.

"Palu," was all Daniel said, a world of meaning in the old childhood name.

Gregory could see understanding in Daniel's eyes before he let go of Gregory's hand and grabbed his arm, pulling Gregory toward a group of people looking at the two of them

10

with undisguised interest. "Come on, let me introduce you to some new friends, and there are some old ones here who will be thrilled to see you again."

"So you've finally decided we are not all bad and are going to grace us with your presence," an amused voice drawled from the middle of the group as they walked up, and Simon Gantry smoothly stepped between two people to stand in front of Gregory.

"Simon," Gregory cried, and shook the offered hand. "How are you?"

"How am I?" Simon said with a laugh. "Well I'm quite all right, seeing as how I've been stuck here in England while you sailed the world, discovering new lands and seducing innocent natives."

Gregory laughed for the first time since arriving in the chilly ballroom. "That would be discovering new plants, and being seduced by natives."

Simon waved his hand airily in front of him with a snort. "The distinction is negligible."

"Not to the plants," Gregory replied seriously, earning another laugh from Simon.

Simon turned then and pulled a voluptuous, chestnut-haired beauty out of the pack. "My dear, let me introduce you to Mr. Gregory Anderson. Gregory, this is Mrs. Neville, Phillip Neville's wife." The lady smiled widely and Gregory bent over to kiss her outstretched hand.

"Mr. Anderson," she said, and her voice was sweet and deep, like dark rum. "I've heard so much about you. And might I add that you live up to your well-deserved reputation."

"My thanks," Gregory replied with a grin. "I think." She appeared to be with child, although her dress masked most of it. Perhaps that was why she seemed to glow with health and exude sensuality.

She laughed just as Phillip Neville and Jonathan Overton stepped up. Neville held out a glass and his wife took it

11

gratefully. Gregory noticed that Overton stood at her other side, his hand on her arm proprietarily. So, he had read Daniel's letter correctly. The three were together. Interesting.

"Anderson," Overton said somberly, shaking his hand. Then he grinned, and Gregory was struck by the difference in him. He had always been serious to the point of morbidity. Neville and his beautiful wife seemed to have brought about a miraculous change. "It's good to see you again. When did you return?"

"In London, only yesterday," he replied, realizing that he'd be repeating it all night. "But we docked at Liverpool over a month ago. I paid my respects to my aunt and uncle and cousins before coming here." He shook his head with disbelief. "And somehow Wilchester got wind of it and sent round an invitation. Where is the happy couple?"

To say Gregory had been shocked to receive an invitation to the ball the Earl of Wilchester was giving to celebrate the marriage of his nephew Ian Witherspoon was an understatement. When he had arrived at his London townhouse to find the invitation he thought surely there was a mistake. But the earl, a patron of the Royal Society, had included a handwritten message urging him to come. He could hardly refuse.

"Dancing around somewhere," a feminine voice said from behind him, with no little disgruntlement. "Apparently we are all expected to dance our feet off."

"Very," another woman's voice said quietly.

Gregory turned to see Kate Collier…no, it was Lady Randall now…standing a few feet away, smiling at him. She was still arrestingly beautiful with her white-blonde hair.

"Lady Randall," he said, stepping toward her at the same time she stepped forward.

Her smile was genuine. "Mr. Anderson, how delightful to see you again."

"My congratulations on the birth of your son," Gregory said.

Lady Randall beamed. "Thank you. Yes, Anthony. He's a delight. But I must say a baby has turned the house on its head." She laughed as she turned to the woman standing behind her and pulled her forward. She was young, but it was clear that she was going to lead some man a merry chase very soon. Tall, slim, shapely, with lustrous dark hair and eyes that snapped with intelligence and deviltry, the young lady's gaze traveled up and down his person with obvious admiration. "May I introduce my niece, Miss Thomas?" Lady Randall said.

The young woman curtsied gracefully, somehow managing to keep her eyes on him the whole time. "How do you do, Mr. Anderson," she drawled with a flirtatious grin. "It is absolutely *delightful* to make your acquaintance."

Gregory bowed from a safe distance. He preferred to admire her type from afar. Alluring and just spreading her wings to begin exploring the games men and women played. He didn't venture into those waters if he could avoid them. "Miss Thomas," he replied politely.

The young beauty spotted someone in the crowd behind him and her eyes lit up like stars fallen from the skies. For a moment Gregory was a little put out, hypocritical though it may be. But relief chased those feelings away. He wouldn't have to worry about pursuit from this quarter.

"Hello, Anderson," Wolf Tarrant said, and Gregory couldn't hide his surprise. Kensington was nowhere to be seen, and it was clear that Wolf's presence around Miss Thomas was proprietary. Things had changed a great deal in his prolonged absence.

Miss Thomas scooted up to Tarrant's side and tucked her hand around his arm. "Several of us attended a lecture at the Royal Society last month, Mr. Anderson, that was based on your latest pamphlet from the Pacific."

Lady Randall moved to stand next to her niece with a subtle shake of her head. Miss Thomas let go of Tarrant reluctantly. It was amusing how alike the two women were in looks and temperament. There was affection between them, but clearly Lady Randall wasn't too happy with the chit's obvious favoritism. Through it all Tarrant remained cool and distant, but his eyes followed Miss Thomas as she stepped around her aunt and put some distance between them.

"Did you?" Gregory replied, bringing everyone back to the conversation.

"Oh, yes," Lady Randall answered. "We were quite popular because we knew you personally." She laughed. "Although I must say Dr. Appleton was disappointed to find out that we were woefully ignorant of your research."

"Anderson?" Gregory felt a hand on his shoulder. He turned and Ian Witherspoon was standing there, grinning at him.

"Gregory!" Ian laughed. He threw an arm around his shoulder and hugged him. "It is you! Did you come all the way from the South Seas to wish me well?"

Gregory laughed with him. "Hardly. I'm here to study the mating patterns of the native English aristocracy," he joked.

One of the only Englishmen who could look Gregory in the eye walked up and glared at him. "Don't even think about setting up an observation post at our house, Anderson," Derek Knightly growled. "I shall have to skin you alive and eat you like one of your islanders." Ian pulled away from Gregory to stand next to Knightly and Gregory was struck again by Ian's blond elegance against Derek's dark, ruffian good looks. He was a bit surprised to see the two still together after Witherspoon's marriage.

"Well, I'm told I taste rather good," Gregory replied benignly, and most of the men laughed. He belatedly realized that Miss Thomas and Lady Randall were still standing there and he blushed.

Miss Thomas smiled wickedly at him and then turned hot eyes on Tarrant, who just motioned behind her. A young gentleman stood there, mouth agape. He was flanked by Jason Randall and Tony Richards. Miss Thomas sighed like the put-upon heroine of a gothic novel. "I suppose you're here to claim a dance?" she asked with ill-disguised irritation. She looked at her dance card. "Mr. Rutherford? Is that right?"

"Very," Jason Randall growled warningly.

Miss Thomas ignored Randall as she curtsied with a polite smile and held out her hand to her poor unwanted dance partner, who stumbled through an apology, although Gregory wasn't sure for what, and led her off. Gregory watched with fascination as she turned to look longingly at Tarrant, who was watching her like a bird of prey seeing his latest meal stolen away from under his nose.

"Hello, Anderson," Tony said warmly. "It has been too long." He shook Gregory's hand with affection. "We have all followed your journeys with great interest."

Just then the Earl of Wilchester walked up with yet another stunningly beautiful woman on his arm. Good lord, had Englishwomen gotten more attractive since he'd left? Or was he just starved for anything English? That thought was a little depressing, since he himself was barely considered English by most of his countrymen.

"Anderson," the earl said with a nod in his direction. "Good of you to come on such short notice. I hope your voyage home was a good one?"

Gregory bowed slightly. "Yes, thank you, sir. Fair weather and calm seas."

"Good, good," the earl said with a polite smile. He turned to his nephew and the smile grew to one of genuine affection. "I am returning your bride, Ian. She could not be parted from you any longer." As an afterthought he turned back to Gregory. "So sorry, Anderson. You haven't met my dear niece, have you?" His affection for the young woman on his arm was obvious. "My dear, let me introduce you to the famous Mr. Gregory Anderson. His father was the renowned naturalist Gordon Anderson, who sailed with Captain James Cook. And his mother was a native of the Friendly Islands. He is," he

15

looked at Gregory as if for confirmation, "a bit of a famous naturalist himself these days, eh?"

Gregory merely smiled politely. He knew lineage was important to these people, the ballroom filled with the cream of the English aristocracy. He should be used to feeling like the ill-bred oddity among them, a curiosity his father had brought home from his explorations. But his stomach felt uneasy, and his smile was forced.

Mrs. Witherspoon held out her hand shyly, a blush staining her cheeks, nearly drowning out the freckles there. "How do you do, Mr. Anderson?" she spoke softly. "I have heard so much of you from Ian and Derek, and Very could not stop talking about the lecture she attended last month." If possible her blush deepened. "I am sorry that I couldn't attend with her." Her dark auburn hair flamed in the candlelight and she bit her lip nervously as if expecting a setdown. From him? Could she not see him in the dim light of the ballroom? He was hardly one to criticize.

Derek stepped forward, a scowl on his face, and Gregory remembered what she had just said. She had heard so much about him from Ian *and* Derek. He shook his head with a small laugh. What on earth had happened to prudish England while he'd been gone? Derek's scowl deepened and Gregory looked over to see Ian and the earl glaring at him. He realized he'd been silent too long.

He stepped forward and took Mrs. Witherspoon's hand in his, smiling broadly before he politely kissed it.

"I am not sorry," he told her firmly, "because now I shall be able to bore you at length in person with my latest discoveries." She smiled timidly at him. "My congratulations on your marriage, madam. I wish you good luck." He looked askance at Ian and then Derek, and turned back to her with a commiserating shake of his head. "You shall need it."

She laughed then, a trill of feminine delight that made Derek's eyes darken as he looked at her with pride and possession. Gregory was so shocked at that look he gaped in astonishment.

Ian stepped up and took her hand from Gregory and placed it on his arm. "Thank you, uncle," he said, the same pride and possession in his voice that Gregory had seen in Derek's face. Mrs. Witherspoon gazed up at Ian with adoration, and then bestowed the same look on Derek. Gregory could almost feel how much she wanted to grasp Derek's arm as well. The earl cleared his throat, breaking the spell.

"Yes, well, that's an excellent idea, Anderson," he boomed a little too loudly. "Sophie and Ian must have a reception for you. It is the perfect introduction for Sophie as a hostess. Now that you are no longer in mourning for your brother, my dear, you can have a small fête." Mrs. Witherspoon paled noticeably.

"I'm not sure I'm up to anything grand, Mrs. Witherspoon," Gregory rushed in to say. "I've only just returned home to England, and am having a bit of a time reacquainting myself with the customs here." He smiled self-deprecatingly. "We wouldn't want the native to forget his manners in front of society, would we?"

Mrs. Witherspoon's brow furrowed as she regarded him soberly. "I am quite sure that we have no need to fear any such thing, Mr. Anderson," she assured him quietly. "And were a slip to occur, handsome and brilliant will often overrule manners." She looked tellingly at Derek, who shrugged innocently.

Gregory was amused by the byplay. "Yes, well, you are too kind, Mrs. Witherspoon."

"Hmm," she replied with a smile. "Sometimes I think so, too."

Her sly candor delighted Gregory. Where had Ian found her? Ian *and* Derek, he amended.

Just then Brett Haversham walked up. "Good God, Anderson!" he cried. "What ill-tide brings you back to our shores? Old Nick must be skating on the ice." Gregory shook his hand, looking at the petite woman on his arm. She had wildly curling dark hair surrounding a sweet face with eyes as full of mischief as the dancing Miss Thomas'. On her other arm was a tall, gorgeous, redheaded man. He had a regal bearing, an amused expression, and blue eyes that Gregory thought he could get lost in. Brett turned to them both. "Let me introduce you to my—" He stopped suddenly and cleared his throat, blushing. "That is to say, may I introduce the Duke of Ashland and his wife?"

Gregory could only laugh in utter delight. Oh, yes, he was going to enjoy this new England.

Chapter Two

ର

"So then Ian and Derek and Sophie were married," Simon told him as they stood on the balcony with Daniel in the cool evening air enjoying a drink and a respite from the heat of the ballroom.

Gregory had been here for over an hour already, but the time had flown by as he caught up with old friends and made new ones. He'd never been so relaxed before at a social gathering. But he'd been insulated tonight from the malicious Hardingtons in attendance, surrounded by people who seemed to accept him as one of them. It was a new and exhilarating experience. Not even during the war had he experienced this level of acceptance from his fellow soldiers. But then again, he'd been caught up in his own dramas then, and may not have noticed their sympathies.

"No, no," Daniel corrected Simon. "Technically, Ian married Sophie. But you are forgetting that Valentine and Kurt married Leah before Ian and Sophie were married."

Gregory looked at them both incredulously. "Valentine and Kurt are married as well? Together?"

Daniel nodded with a wry grin. "Yes, so be careful. This happiness seems to be contagious."

Gregory waved his drink at Daniel and then Simon. "But the two of you have not been afflicted?"

Simon snuggled up to Daniel's side and laid his head upon the shorter man's shoulder. "Who's to say we're not very happy together?" he twittered in a grating falsetto.

"Me," Daniel replied with a shove, and Simon just laughed as he danced out of reach as Daniel tried to cuff him on the head.

Gregory was amused by their antics, but his attention was snagged by a couple inside the ballroom. He could see them through the open French doors. They waltzed by oblivious to everyone around them, or so he thought. But as they danced by the door they both turned and their eyes met his. They had arrived a short time ago, before Gregory had stepped out. He'd watched them as they descended the stairs into the ballroom. She was small and dainty, with generous breasts. Her hair was blonde, that gorgeous shade of yellow that only Englishwomen seemed to be able to grow. Golden and buttery, it cascaded around her head in a riot of natural curls, similar to Gregory's. But hers looked as if it would be soft and smooth to the touch. The pale blue of her dress only seemed to highlight the pale perfection of her skin. Her face was a delectable little heart, sharp chin and round cheeks with a tilted nose and wide, innocent eyes.

Her husband, for Gregory had no doubt that's who he was, was tall and well built. He looked like a Corinthian, perhaps. Light brown hair, almost a dark blond, was cut close to his head in a fashionable Brutus. The hair that brushed along his wide forehead drew Gregory's gaze to his face. He had brows lighter than his hair above eyes small and wide-set with a slight uptilt to them. His face was long, as was his nose. The bridge was thin and the end sharp. It was a very English nose. Gregory got the impression that he smiled often. Together the man and his wife seemed so…English. And yet there was something exotic about them. Was it the way they moved, so in tune with one another? Each touch was a caress, each look was filled with longing. What was it he found so intriguing about them?

He watched as a tall, elegant man approached them and they stopped dancing. With a start, Gregory realized it was Hardington. He watched the husband shake his head and he and Hardington exchanged what looked to be unpleasant words while his wife moved to stand behind him and looked out at the balcony, at Gregory.

20

"Hello? Gregory?"

Simon's amused voice brought Gregory out of his reverie and he realized that he was openly staring, and that the couple stood in the doorway, staring back, Hardington gone.

"Ah, I see you've noticed Nat and Alecia." Daniel's voice dripped with wry amusement. "Would you care for an introduction?"

"You know them?" Gregory asked, unable to look away. Were they looking at him as hungrily as he was looking at them? He'd been desperately hoping to find someone while he was here in England. It had been so damn long since he'd fucked someone who was more than a warm body. He wanted intelligent conversation, lusty appetites, witty remarks, hungry mouths and hands. He wanted to be explored, discovered, plundered. He wanted someone to make him theirs if only for a short time, until he left again. Because he would leave. He didn't belong here any more than he belonged in his mother's land.

"Yes. We all know them." At Simon's offhand remark Gregory tore his gaze from the couple and glared at Simon.

"What does that mean?" His angry question surprised him. Surely he didn't think he was the first man to draw their eye? He wasn't the kind that tempted people from the straight and narrow. Only intrepid souls who had ventured into passion's dark waters before came his way. He was too different, an outsider, a stranger, a curiosity to be studied and examined before putting it back on the shelf.

"Not apparently what you think." Daniel spoke calmly, his smooth voice soothing Gregory's confusing anger. "They are simply our true friends here in London." Gregory raised a brow inquiringly. "Surely you know that the liaisons among our friends are not accepted. They maintain a subdued presence in society, but everyone knows what is really going on. Very few cut them directly. But most people maintain a wary, disapproving distance." He shrugged. "Nat and Alecia do not. They are friends." Daniel waved them over. "I think you will like them."

Was the man mad? Like them? Gregory almost laughed aloud at how tame the word sounded compared to the wild feelings that were coursing through him as the couple approached. If he had his way, he'd be fucking them before the night was through.

Nat couldn't believe their luck. Daniel was waving them over. It looked as if he wanted to introduce them to the man they'd been watching since they walked into the ballroom. Who was he? He was bloody, fucking amazing.

"Oh my God, Nat," Alecia whispered. "I think he wants to meet us."

"I think I want to fuck him," Nat whispered back. Alecia laughed as he'd known she would. "I'm serious, Lee," he told her.

"I know," she chuckled. "It's just that I was thinking the same thing." They laughed together for a moment, and she sounded breathless. Hell, so did he. "He's gorgeous, isn't he? Even more so the closer we get."

Gorgeous did not do him justice. He was a giant, several inches over six feet surely. His shoulders were the widest Nat had ever seen. His skin was exotic, with just a hint of brown color kissed by the sun. His hair was black, thick and curly, longer than was fashionable. It was parted in the middle and brushed back, but it defied efforts to tame it. It looked rough, and Nat shivered as he imagined the other man rubbing that hair on his thighs as he leaned down to suck Nat's cock. Oh, please, Nat prayed, if there is a God let him make this man want me.

His features were mesmerizing. Nat had never seen anyone like him. He had a broad, flat nose and a pair of deep-set, intense eyes. His mouth made Nat tremble. It was wide, with generous lips, full and luscious. Nat wanted to kiss that mouth. He wanted to see it wrapped around his cock. He wanted to see those lips suckling Alecia's breasts and teasing her cunt with kisses. Christ, he had to stop this fantasizing. He was going to embarrass them all in these tight breeches.

What if he didn't like men? What if he didn't like the idea of being the third in their bed? Not all men liked that. They were willing to fuck Alecia. But that wasn't what Nat and Alecia wanted. That wasn't what they liked. They liked to share, plain and simple. Not very often, only a handful of times. But they liked to share someone, they didn't want someone to share them. It was a fine line, but it was their line. When they took someone to their bed it was about Nat and Alecia and what they wanted. Would this giant agree to those terms? And if he didn't, would they take him to their bed anyway? Nat thought that perhaps they might, because he was that tempting.

Alecia's hand tightened on his arm as they drew near the three men waiting for them on the balcony. Nat and Daniel had been lovers soon after Nat and Alecia had been married. But only once. When Daniel found out Nat was married he was livid. It had taken time, and Alecia's forgiveness, for Daniel to speak to him again. Nat still shook his head in wonder at how selfish and immature he'd been then. He'd hurt Alecia so much in the early years of their marriage. He'd driven her into the arms of other men, and the hurt and confusion between them had almost caused an irreparable rift.

He looked over at Simon with affection. It was Simon who had changed everything. Simon who had made them grow up and learn to love one another. He'd been the first one, the first man they shared, and it had been Simon's idea. In Simon's arms they learned to love and please one another. Nat would be forever grateful to the other man for giving him back his wife.

"Daniel, Simon," Nat greeted them with a nod. "How are you?" The stranger was staring at him and Alecia. Nat felt the hair on his nape rise with awareness, felt the perspiration on

23

his scalp and under his arms as his cock twitched and grew, just from that gaze.

"May I present Nathaniel and Alecia Digby," Daniel drawled, and Nat saw Simon hiding a knowing grin behind his glass.

"Hello, Daniel," Alecia said warmly. "Simon, dear, how are you?" Simon leaned over and kissed Alecia's cheek, and then he whispered something in her ear that made her blush and her eyes widen as she looked at the tall stranger.

"Oh, my," she said breathlessly. She looked at the stranger with that mix of innocent trust and lustful hunger that never failed to drive Nat mad, a fierce blush staining her cheeks. "Simon says that you would like to go home with us," she told him, and Nat nearly choked on his astonishment. "Can we learn your name first, or is that a great secret only shared with a few?"

The stranger's smile was as hungry and open and Alecia's. "My name is Gregory Anderson. If you wish to know more, there is a price." His voice was deep. Nat had expected some sort of foreign accent, but he sounded very British.

Nat cleared his throat, and to his eternal gratitude the man turned a gaze as hungry and delighted on him as it had been on Alecia. His eyes were a rich, deep, dark brown. "A price?" Nat said, a little embarrassed by the tremor of desire in his voice. But only a little. Gregory Anderson's smile deepened as he nodded. "And what might that be?" Nat inquired, beginning to enjoy the game.

Mr. Anderson tilted his head, and Nat noticed that he had just a touch of gray hair at his temples, lost amid the curls there. He was older than Nat had first thought, then. "That, you will have to discover on the journey," Mr. Anderson declared quietly, and Nat stopped trying to hide his desire. Daniel and Simon were forgotten as Nat devoured the other man with his gaze.

"Then let us begin the journey, by all means," Nat replied. He turned toward the ballroom doors, bringing Alecia with him, and looked over his shoulder. "Are you coming, Mr. Anderson?"

Gregory Anderson walked up to Alecia's other side. "Where you lead, I will follow," he told Nat with a sly grin.

"I thought you were the intrepid explorer on this journey," Alecia teased.

Mr. Anderson grinned as he stopped to let Nat and Alecia precede him through the ballroom door. "Not tonight, my dear Alecia," he murmured. "Tonight I am the territory to be explored."

* * * * *

Alecia's mouth was dry. She licked her lips and Mr. Anderson followed the motion of her tongue with his eyes. She couldn't disguise her breathlessness, either. When he wasn't watching her lick her lips, he seemed mesmerized by the rise and fall of her chest with each deep breath.

She was a puddle of want. Good lord, the man was gorgeous. She couldn't remember ever wanting someone like this. Well, someone besides Nat. And she hadn't wanted him like this since before they were married — since before all the hurt and scandal and fear. Mr. Anderson made her feel like an untried virgin again. As if he had all sorts of wicked things in mind she'd never tried before. And she'd tried quite a bit, truth be told. Sometimes more than she wanted to remember the next morning. But she wanted to make Nat happy. And Nat was happy when she let her inhibitions go and enjoyed her passions. Truthfully, she was rather happy then, too.

She very much wanted to enjoy passion with Mr. Anderson.

And the way he was staring at Nat made Alecia squirm. She loved to watch Nat with another man. There was something so illicit about it, so naughty and divine. Watching Nat fuck a man made Alecia happy. She wasn't sure if that was because she knew how much Nat enjoyed it, or if it just aroused her tremendously. The thought of Nat and Mr. Anderson fucking each other nearly made Alecia swoon right there on the sofa in their drawing room.

"So you are the famous Gregory Anderson, explorer and naturalist?" Alecia asked politely, if a little breathlessly. They were sitting in the drawing room because Alecia wasn't sure how to proceed, and neither was Nat. Once they'd realized who he was, Nat was full of admiration in the carriage, but Alecia had been embarrassed that she hadn't made the connection immediately. And she'd teased him about being an explorer at Wilchester's, too. Now she was overwhelmed and tongue-tied. He was a brilliant naturalist who had seen half the world. She was formally trained in etiquette, not classical literature or the sciences, and had never left England. Surely he would find her lacking if she attempted conversation.

Mr. Anderson had been very quiet on the drive to their townhouse. It was almost as if he were observing them. She felt a little like a scientific specimen under his scrutiny.

"Yes," he answered simply, clearly in no hurry to fill the silence that stretched between them.

Alecia looked at Nat in desperation and he just shrugged.

"I'm not sure what to do here, Mr. Anderson," Alecia ventured tentatively.

"Call me Palu," he interrupted. For a moment he looked startled, as if he'd surprised himself by speaking.

"Palu?" she asked. "Is that Italian?"

He shook his head. "No. It's my name in the language of my mother's people." He seemed to reach a decision of some sort, which in turn seemed to open the floodgates of speech. "My father called me that. It was the name my mother gave me before she died. It is the name I am called in the islands." He stood abruptly, and Nat stood as well.

"All right, Palu," Alecia said, the name strange but exotic sounding in her mouth.

The man was as exotic as his name. He dwarfed their small drawing room. Alecia had feared for the welfare of the small settee upon which he'd sat. At the same time she'd wanted to crawl into his lap, straddle him, and ride him until she screamed. She worried her lip a bit as she stared up at him, wondering if he could read her decidedly wanton thoughts in her face.

He smiled and Alecia relaxed. It was the hungry, relaxed, playful smile he'd given them at Wilchester's. It was desire. Alecia knew what to do with that.

He reached for Alecia's hand and pulled her up from the sofa. She went willingly, letting him lead. It was clear he knew where they were going far better than Nat and Alecia did. He threw his arm around Nat's shoulders, and then gently pulled her against him, too, hugging her with one arm. He began to walk them over to the drawing room door, both of them clasped to his sides and Alecia found that she fell in step with him quite easily.

"Come on," he said jovially.

"Where are we going?" Nat asked, and Alecia heard the laughter and desire in his voice. He wasn't used to being led, she realized. Usually Nat set the pace when they invited another man over.

"I thought you might like to watch me fuck your wife," Palu said happily. Alecia lost a step and his arm tightened around her as he kept moving, holding her up.

"And then?" Nat asked, his voice low and breathless.

"And then she can watch me fuck you," Palu answered matter-of-factly.

They'd reached the drawing room doors and Palu released them to step over and grasp the handles. He turned to look at them over his shoulder with a grin and he waggled his eyebrows, his eyes twinkling.

"Ready?" he asked.

"Oh, yes," Alecia said on a trembling breath, and Palu rewarded her by throwing the doors open and ushering her through.

Chapter Three

ଛା

Nat closed the bedchamber door behind him and Palu turned to see the other man leaning back against the door, regarding him intently. "Everyone calls you Gregory. Why?"

Palu didn't sense any disapproval in his tone, just curiosity. "It is a name they are comfortable with. I suppose it is my real name to them, the name from my father's family, and the name on all the legal documents."

"And yet, to you it is not your real name?"

Nat showed a perception that Palu had not expected. He shook his head. "No. To me it is not my real name."

"We want you to be the real you when you are here with us." Alecia's voice was sweet and tentative and Palu turned to see her sitting on the edge of the bed clutching her hands nervously. "If that is acceptable to you?" When he didn't answer right away she rushed to fill the silence. "I mean, I am comfortable with Palu. Nat?"

"Comfort has nothing to do with it, Alecia," Nat told her with a smile. "He *is* Palu."

"Yes." Palu interrupted before Alecia felt the need to reassure him again. It was sweet, how nervous and unsure she was. "Yes, here I am Palu." Palu felt free, unencumbered by the worries that usually beset him here in England. In the carriage he'd watched Nat and Alecia, and it was clear that they were happily married, perhaps even in love. This was not a whim or some scheme to use him to hurt one another. And now they'd accepted his real name. Perhaps here with them he could let down his guard for a few hours. He could be Palu, and not the Englishman Gregory Anderson. It was so bloody hard sometimes to try to be both. He hadn't had to don his

29

English nature for years. He avoided Englishmen and civilization as much as possible. But for the last month, day in and day out he'd been playing the role and he wanted, no, needed to set it aside for one night. Perhaps if all went well, for two or three nights with Nat and Alecia.

"So, Palu," Nat asked with a wicked gleam in his eye, "are you going to fuck my wife?"

"Yes." His simple answer seemed to please the laughing Englishman.

"Short and to the point. Very good." Nat walked over and slowly circled Palu. After one pass around he put his hand on Palu's shoulder and dragged it across his upper back and down his arm as he circled a second time. The touch left a wake of desire licking at Palu's skin. As he passed in front he stopped and faced Palu, then he unbuttoned Palu's jacket.

"May I?" he asked quietly, with his hands poised in front of Palu's torso. He knew Nat wanted to slide the coat off. He nodded, and Nat placed both hands on his stomach. His muscles involuntarily clenched at the touch and he heard Nat's indrawn breath.

Nat slowly glided his hands up under the lapels and onto Palu's shoulders, and then ran his hands down Palu's arms, pushing the jacket down and off. It fell unheeded to the floor.

"Christ," he whispered, "you're huge."

Palu laughed out loud. "Yes, I am." Again, his simple answer seemed to please Nat.

Nat gazed up at him from under his eyelashes, a sensual, teasing glance. "What do you want me to do, Palu?"

Palu felt as if he was running up hill. His blood was thick in his veins and his heart was pounding in his chest. He could see Nat's hard cock outlined by his tight breeches, and he could hear Alecia's excited breathing from the bed. He looked over at her and she was flushed, her eyes wide and a little wild as she watched her husband touch him.

He couldn't remember the last time he'd been this excited to fuck anyone. He'd never had a man and woman together. Separately, yes, but never two lovers at the same time. He knew just how he was going to do it, however. He'd love sweet little Alecia while Nat watched. He'd eat her pretty pink and white cunt and palm her beautiful breasts. And he knew Nat would not be idle. No, the pretty, laughing Englishman would probably be unable to keep his hands off Palu. But he wouldn't let Nat rush him with Alecia. He wanted to take her slow and deep and hear her moan and cry for him. He knew that it would make Nat mad for him. And after Alecia was well pleasured, Palu would take her laughing, teasing husband hard and fast and rough, because he knew that's what Nat wanted. And Nat would moan and cry, too. And perhaps pretty little Alecia would come again just from watching them.

"I want you both to undress for me," Palu told him with a bit of a growl in his voice. He couldn't help it. He was close to losing his control with these two. It had been too long for him, too long since he'd been wanted like this. He hadn't looked away from Alecia and he saw her close her eyes briefly, as if overcome by the thought of being naked for him. "And then I want the two of you to undress me."

"Do you?" Nat asked softly, a hard edge to his voice. "And if we want something different?"

"That is my price," Palu replied calmly. "The journey begins here."

"It is a small price," Alecia said as she rose from the bed, one hand holding onto the bedpost as if she felt unbalanced. "Surely you value your secrets more?"

"They are mine to sell as I deem fit," he assured her with a grin. "And I would reveal them all to see the two of you naked and awaiting my pleasure."

Nat huffed out a small laugh and Palu turned to see the grin that he was quickly coming to crave. When Nat laughed his eyes crinkled so they were mere slits of sky blue in his face.

Palu found it charming. "Then Alecia is right. It is a small price to pay for all your secrets." He ran his hand teasingly down Palu's chest to his stomach, pulling it away when he reached the top of Palu's breeches. "And I believe that you may have quite a few, Palu."

Palu just grinned back, making Nat laugh again.

Nat beckoned Alecia over and he turned her without a word and began to undo the back of her dress. Palu's heart stuttered in his chest as her dress gaped open over her back. She wore a corset underneath, but he found the intimate scene breathtakingly arousing. It was obvious Nat had undressed his wife many times. He did so efficiently, but each touch was lovingly bestowed, and Nat interspersed his ministrations with kisses and murmured words. Would he undress Palu the same way?

Nat turned slightly and Palu realized that he was deliberately blocking his view of Alecia. For a moment he was alarmed, thinking that perhaps Nat had changed his mind and didn't want him to see his wife naked. But then Nat threw a grin over his shoulder and Palu knew it was just another form of teasing. He found he liked Nat's teasing very much.

"Now don't look," Nat chided him. "I want you to see us both together. Turn around."

He sighed with resignation and turned to face the wall. He heard Alecia giggle from behind Nat. "Very well, but do not keep me waiting too long, Nat," he warned. "I am desperate to fuck the two of you."

"Oh God," Alecia murmured fervently and Palu grinned at the wall in front of him.

He heard clothes rustling behind him.

"Honestly, Nat," Alecia said in exasperation, "must you have your coats cut so tight? It is like peeling an orange."

Palu burst out laughing. "I like the cut of his coat. It shows off his shoulders and small waist to perfection."

He heard Nat chuckle. "You see, Alecia? He was enamored of the cut of my coat. If I had my tailor alter it as you wish, Palu would not be chomping at the bit to fuck you, my pretty."

"Oh, and I suppose the neckline of my gown had nothing to do with attracting his interest?" Alecia teased right back. "It wasn't your waist he was staring at half the night."

"I confess that I found you both irresistible," Palu assured them. "Now may I please see what all those clothes were hiding?"

"Turn around," Nat told him roughly.

If Palu thought he had wanted before, he'd been a fool. Nat stood behind Alecia and slightly off to the side so Palu could see the uninterrupted line of his body from shoulder to toes on the right side. Alecia was tucked in close to him, one of her hands resting on Nat's against her bare stomach. Her other hand reached behind her and grasped Nat's hip. Nat cupped one large breast in his hand, and as Palu watched he ran his thumb lightly over her pale pink nipple and both men watched it pucker and darken. Palu let his eyes wander, his blood heating at the sight of her soft belly and the blonde curls between her legs. She was perfection. His mouth watered at the thought of tasting every delectable inch of her.

After memorizing every line of Alecia's body, Palu turned his examination on Nat. The first thing he noticed was that Nat's shoulders were covered with freckles. He wanted to taste those, too. Could you feel them on your tongue? Nat's skin wasn't a clear porcelain like Alecia's, but it still gleamed pink and white in the candlelight. He had lean, hard muscles, a heavy chest lightly dusted with hair and a tight stomach, thighs thick with muscles and a well-turned calf. They were beautiful, every English inch of them.

"Well?" Nat asked wryly, "have you stopped speaking again?"

"You are beautiful, both of you," he answered. There were no other words. He was extremely aroused at the thought of having these two lovers. They were so obviously in love with one another. To be allowed to share that, for even one night, was a gift.

"Palu," Alecia whispered, and when he looked at her he could see in her eyes that she understood what he couldn't say.

"Will you let your hair down?" he asked, hoping she would. He wanted to wrap his big, brown fist in her bright curls.

She nodded and let go of Nat to take the pins out of her hair one by one. Nat held out his hand and she deposited them in his open palm as she took them out. Again the intimacy of it struck Palu. When she was done she shook her head and Nat stepped away to empty his palm onto the top of the dressing table.

Palu watched Nat as he turned to walk back to Alecia. Nat's cock was hard, curving up toward his belly from a crotch full of curly hair, darker than the hair on his head. His rod was pink and white, like the rest of him, the head a darker, mouthwatering pink. He wasn't overly large, but he was pretty, and Palu was quite sure that Nat knew how to use his cock very well.

"Do you like it?" Nat asked quietly. He had stopped and now just stood there letting Palu look.

Palu nodded. "Yes. That was going to be my next request. I wanted to see all of you."

He saw Nat's chest and stomach quiver as he took a deep breath, and when Palu looked at his face he was flushed, his eyes small and intense, slitted with desire now, not laughter.

"All you had to do was ask," Nat told him, his voice deep and slow. Palu liked his voice. Hell, he liked everything about Nat.

He nodded. "I was going to."

This time Nat did laugh, and then he walked back over to Alecia. He wrapped both arms around Alecia's waist and rested his chin on her shoulder, frowning at Palu. "You are wearing too many clothes."

He nodded, all the old fears rising in his chest. Would they still want him when they saw the secrets he hid under his English clothes? He never looked more savage than when he was naked. But for some inexplicable reason he wanted very much to reveal that side of himself to these two. He only prayed that they still found him acceptable when he did.

Nat watched Palu's expressive face. The other man couldn't hide much of what he was thinking, or perhaps he simply didn't try to hide it. Either way, Nat enjoyed the pleasure he'd seen on Palu's face as he'd stared at him and Alecia, the hunger in his gaze when he'd seen Nat's cock. He liked how open Palu was, how eager. God, Nat wanted to fuck him. He wanted to see the other man's face as Nat filled him. But first things first.

"It's our job to undress you, isn't it?" Nat asked, trying to keep his tone light and conversational. Fair was fair, after all. Palu had seen them and now it was time for recompense.

"Come." The big man beckoned slowly. "Come and strip me."

Nat started to walk over, but stopped when Alecia didn't immediately follow. He turned back to her with a frown and saw her watching Palu, nervously biting her lip. Nat knew she did that when she was worried about something. He looked back at Palu and saw him drop his hand and tilt his head to stare at Alecia.

"What is it, my love?" Nat asked.

"I just..." Alecia swallowed nervously, "I just want to make sure that Palu understands what we want. The two of us, I mean. And that he wants the same thing."

The burst of laughter from Palu was unexpected and both Nat and Alecia were startled.

"My dear Alecia," Palu told her with a wide grin, "you have no idea how much I want this. I'm sorry, the words don't come easily for me. But yes, yes I want you both beneath me, on top of me, touching me, fucking me. This is what I want. *You* are what I want. Never doubt that."

"I don't fuck other men," Alecia said hesitantly, looking over at Nat. He nodded at her, encouraging her to continue. Nat hadn't said anything before because he wasn't sure what Alecia wanted tonight. He knew she wanted Palu. And surprisingly, he didn't think he'd object if she chose to break this unwritten rule of their affairs with Palu.

Palu looked between them for a moment, his face shockingly unreadable. So he'd deliberately chosen not to hide earlier, Nat realized. Then Palu nodded. "That is fair. Whatever you two want, I will do."

Alecia let out a breath as if she'd been holding it. "All right, then. I just wanted to be sure." She laughed then, sounding quite relieved. "What a strange night this has been! I don't believe I've ever had an encounter like it."

It was an offhand remark, but it struck Nat to the core. No, they'd never had an encounter like it. Usually Nat arranged for their men and orchestrated the evening. Tonight had been spontaneous, unexpected, a headlong rush into adventure with an exotic stranger. And Nat knew he would never regret the impulsive desire that had brought this man to their bed.

"The journey has only just begun," Palu told her with a grin. "We have much more territory to explore before we reach our destination."

Alecia laughed and Nat grinned. He liked the sound of that.

"And you?" Palu had turned to Nat. "Do you fuck other men?"

Nat nodded, and couldn't stop his grin from turning to one of anticipation. "Oh yes."

Palu grinned back. "Good."

When they walked over to Palu the atmosphere was considerably lighter than it had been. Nat was glad. He wanted a lighthearted night instead of the somber, intense couplings he and Alecia usually found with other men. Rarely were their partners jovial or playful. For the first time since Simon, Nat was looking forward to not just rutting, but being with a particular man. With Palu.

Nat knew that there were dangers lurking around this night. He liked Palu perhaps too much. He wasn't looking for an emotional attachment to anyone else. He had Alecia. He loved her. They were man and wife, best friends, and that was all he wanted. He knew their friends enjoyed marriages among three, but Nat had never desired it. He liked to fuck men, but he didn't want to love one. How difficult that was. He'd seen it. Seen them all have to deny their feelings among polite society, seen the hurt and pain and ostracism that love like that visited upon its victims. No, he didn't want to do that. He didn't want to hurt anyone else whom he loved.

"Don't frown, pretty Nat," Palu said, and he put his large, rough, hot palm against the back of Nat's neck and pulled Nat to him. Palu buried his face in the curve of Nat's shoulder, rubbing his nose against him before he kissed the pulse beating heavily in his neck.

"Damn," Nat murmured, swamped by lust at the feel of Palu's mouth on him, the size of his hand against Nat's neck. Palu chuckled and pulled again, until Nat took that last step that pressed his naked body against Palu's fully clothed one. Palu's heat soaked through his clothes, warming Nat. He had to gulp in a breath and swallow deeply to keep his knees from buckling at the eroticism of it.

"Undress me," Palu whispered against him, and Nat could only nod.

Palu let go of him and Nat took an unsteady step back. Alecia was standing there with a smile on her face.

"That good?" she teased.

"Yes," was all Nat said, and she and Palu laughed.

"Nat," Palu growled, and Nat knew what he wanted.

Nat reached for his cravat and untied it. He had a devil of a time. "Your man certainly knows how to tie these," he complained as he struggled with the starched linen.

"Feel free to cut it off," Palu said in disgust. "I hate them."

"All men say that," Alecia laughed as she stepped behind Palu to smooth her hands over his back and upper arms. She hummed with delight.

Nat finally got the cravat undone and threw it down. Palu's shirt fell open nearly to his waist and Nat thought he glimpsed something on Palu's chest. He glanced up and saw Palu watching him intently.

Nat pulled the shirt from out of Palu's breeches and then very slowly slid his hands underneath to Palu's bare stomach. The skin was smooth and hot and Nat just let his hands rest there for a moment, enjoying it. Suddenly Palu groaned and arched his neck, and Nat pushed the shirt up to see Alecia's hands sliding around Palu's waist from the back, her nails scratching his skin. Nat continued to push the shirt up and Palu grabbed the bottom and pulled it off in one quick motion, then threw it down and lowered his arms.

Nat stood frozen. Palu had elaborate drawings covering his upper right arm and shoulder. It was a complicated design of black swirls and patterns of dots and lines with a heavy black band perhaps two inches thick drawn around his biceps. As he watched Palu flexed his arm and the muscle bulged, tightening the band and giving the illusion that the swirls moved along his arm. The upper portion of the design ran over his shoulder onto his chest. Suddenly Nat knew what it was.

"I've read about this," he said in wonder, reaching out to Palu's arm. He hesitated and Palu moved his arm, indicating that Nat could touch it. When he did he expected to be able to feel the design, but he couldn't. The skin was as smooth and hot as the rest of Palu. "It's *tatau*."

"Yes," Palu said, and Nat sensed rather than heard his wariness. "It is *tatatau* in my mother's world, *moko* to others."

Alecia was running her hands over Palu's arm, her delight evident. "It's beautiful, Palu," she exclaimed. "Is it a drawing?"

"Yes and no," Palu said, relaxing under Alecia's hands. "It is native ink made in the islands just for this purpose. They cut the skin with a small comb or chisel and rub the ink into it to make a permanent mark."

Alecia gasped. "But that must have been incredibly painful! It is beautiful, but it sounds so dangerous, Palu."

Palu laughed and Nat felt a catch in his stomach that he decided to ignore. He was allowed to like Palu, to find him irresistible. It didn't mean he was going to fall in love. Even if the *tataus* were the most beautiful thing he had ever seen.

"They were incredibly painful, pretty Alecia. But they are important in the Pacific, among my mother's people in The Friendly Islands. They prove that you are a man, that you can take the pain. If I had not gotten them, I would have been considered a coward."

Nat couldn't resist any longer. He leaned down and licked a path along one of the complicated swirls of the *tatau*.

"You like them?" Palu asked in a husky voice.

It was Nat's turn to laugh. "Like them? I plan to lick every inch of them."

Palu grinned down at him. "Good. Because there are more."

39

Alecia was shocked. She admitted it. She had never seen anything like it. Palu had the *tatau* on his arse. They'd stripped his pants off in record time when he told them he had more of the beautiful designs. But they hadn't expected this.

"It looks like you're wearing short pants," she said in wonder. The *tatau* on his behind actually covered him all over from his waist to above his knees. The design was similar to the one on his arm, although it was heavier here, covering nearly every inch of skin.

"This is the traditional male *tatatau* in parts of the South Seas," Palu explained. "I was afraid at first, and so got the one on my arm. But after surviving that, I decided to get this. I wasn't accepted until I did."

Alecia fell to her knees behind him to get a better look, and Nat joined her. Together they ran their hands over the beautiful black ink designs. Giant black swirls covered the cheeks of his buttocks and then ran up to his lower back and down onto his legs. Without any hesitation Alecia shoved at a leg, forcing Palu to widen his stance.

"They're on the inside, too," she gasped. She grasped his thigh in both hands, and then ran one up onto his firm, muscular bottom.

"That feels good," Palu moaned.

Alecia looked over to see Nat licking a path across Palu's other cheek, following a swirl. The sight was so arousing Alecia actually felt the moisture rush from her sex.

"Nat," she whispered, mesmerized. Nat opened his eyes to look at her and then softly bit Palu's cheek.

"Damn, yes," Palu groaned.

Nat grinned and licked the place he had bitten, making Palu moan again.

"He's rather noisy, isn't he?" Nat asked Alecia, and there was something in his voice she'd rarely heard before when they were with someone else, something hot and intimate that they only shared with one another. Yet Alecia couldn't mind it. She wanted to share that with Palu, too.

Alecia moved to Palu's front, still on her knees. The *tatau* was on his stomach and hips and legs, and Alecia moaned when she saw that it covered his cock as well. And it was a fat, beautiful, full cock. His brown skin and the *tatau* made it appear purple with arousal, and Alecia could see a heavy vein pulsing along the underside. The head was as thick as the staff, weeping with desire, and suddenly all Alecia wanted to do in this life was take that cock in her mouth and taste it.

"His cock has it, too," she told Nat in a trembling voice.

"Bloody fucking hell," Nat groaned, and he crawled around to kneel next to Alecia. "Now that had to hurt," Nat commented breathlessly.

Palu chuckled and he sounded as breathless as she and Nat. "Yes." He reached down and gently tugged at Alecia's hair, forcing her to look up at him. His dark eyes shone brightly, his cheeks were flushed, and he had a dimple in his cheek as he smiled sweetly at her. A dimple. Oh God, she was lost. "I want you to kiss it, pretty Alecia," he whispered roughly. He closed his fist slowly in her hair and pulled her forward and up. With a glad cry, Alecia let him.

"Yes, Palu," she agreed, trembling with anticipation. "Yes, I want to do that, too."

She opened her mouth and Palu slid inside, and Alecia moaned at the hot, wicked taste of him. He was so thick in her mouth, she could barely take him. But once he was inside she sucked and licked and enjoyed him, so much.

"Lee," Nat choked out, and she panicked. Nat had never wanted her to do this to another man before. She'd never wanted to. It was so intimate and personal, and she put herself at Palu's mercy when she did it. She had never trusted anyone but Nat to fuck her mouth. But when she'd seen Palu's cock, and he had asked so sweetly, she hadn't thought about it.

41

She'd just reacted, just taken him, taken what she wanted. She started to pull off reluctantly but Nat stopped her.

"No!" he cried out. Suddenly Nat was behind her, his legs straddling hers, his cheek pressed against hers, as he watched. He was panting heavily, his arousal a hot brand against her bottom. He held on to her elbows as she grasped Palu's thighs to hold her upright.

"Yes," Palu hissed, and his hand tightened in her hair. But it didn't hurt, he wouldn't hurt her. She knew he wouldn't. Very gently he pulled out just a few inches, and then he pressed back into her mouth. It was too much, he was too thick, and she whimpered in distress.

"I'm sorry," Palu gasped. "I won't move again, I swear it. Just don't stop, Alecia. What you're doing to me, it's enough." He laughed shakily. "It's more than enough."

Alecia suckled his cock, and she felt the shudder that racked his big, strong body. She felt powerful here at his feet. Not weak, not threatened. But powerful with the trust that Palu placed in her.

"Lee," Nat whispered again, and then she saw him lean over and lick the *tatau* on Palu's cock, following a swirl down to where her mouth hugged him. Palu groaned and reached down a hand to rest it on Nat's head as he licked and nibbled the base of Palu's cock. Palu shuddered again with a moan.

Nat's arms wrapped around Alecia and he hummed his approval, of the taste or of Palu's reaction Alecia wasn't sure. He thrust his hard cock against her and sucked gently on Palu's shaft. Alecia loved the sounds he made on Palu's cock. She slid her hands up Palu's thighs and slipped one between his legs, and then she lightly cupped his testicles.

"Stop," Palu ground out, and Alecia pulled her hand back as if burned. Palu tugged gently on her hair and she slowly let him slide out of her mouth.

"Please, don't make us stop," Nat whispered, nuzzling his nose into the dark, curly hair at Palu's groin. Alecia found the sight of Nat there devastatingly sensual. His white skin against Palu's dark skin and hair and *tataus* made Palu seem even more exotic, more strange and unknown and delightful.

"Is that what you want?" Palu asked them softly. "For me to come with your mouths? Or do you want me to fuck you?"

Alecia imagined Palu's thick cock with its foreign *tataus* fucking into her and she got lightheaded. Her sex throbbed and the muscles of her passage clenched in anticipation.

Palu cupped her cheek and tipped her head up. He was looking at her tenderly, but there was an edge of desperation in his eyes and the set of his mouth. "You want that, don't you, Alecia?"

She bit her lip in indecision, but finally shook her head in the negative. "I can't," she whispered.

Palu sighed, but he smiled gently at her. "Will you let me touch you? Kiss you?"

"Please, Palu," she whispered, and the gratitude and satisfaction that flashed across his face was worth everything to her at that moment.

Chapter Four

ೞ

Palu sat on the bed, his back resting on the wooden frame against the wall. His dark skin and *tatau* were framed in stark relief by the white bed linens. He liked it. He liked how he looked here, as if on display for their pleasure. No one else had seen the *tatau* here in England — just Nat and Alecia. And they liked them. Palu grinned as Nat crawled up his legs like a cat, licking the swirls on his thigh. Correction, they loved them.

Alecia climbed onto the bed beside him and then she straddled his lap. Palu held her hands as she settled over him. He rested his head against the wall closing his eyes in pleasure as he felt the moist heat of her cunt hovering over his cock at the same time Nat's clever tongue painted wet patterns on his *tatau*. When she didn't move, Palu lifted his head to look at her.

"Good," she purred. "I like it when you watch me." She bit her lip, as if unsure. She was a puzzle, shy and wanton at the same time.

Palu chuckled. "I like it when you watch me, too." He tilted his head and studied the desire written on her face. She wanted him. She might not be willing to fuck him, and he had to respect her decision to only fuck her husband, but she wanted him.

"I want to watch you touch me," Alecia whispered. She played the siren, but Palu saw her cheeks turn pink with embarrassment as she spoke.

Nat groaned from behind Alecia. "Christ, I want to watch that, too. Hold on." Nat tumbled off Palu's legs and scooted up. He lay on his side next to Palu, his arm bent and his head resting on his hand. "All right, do it."

Alecia laughed and seemed to relax and Palu grinned down at Nat, who was staring at his cock and Alecia's sex, which were directly at his eye level, with wicked delight.

"Do you always enjoy watching a man pleasure your wife so much?" Palu asked as he grabbed Alecia's delicate hips in his large hands. He could feel the bones under her soft skin and it reminded him how small she was. He had to be careful so he didn't hurt her. Nat didn't answer right away and Palu paused to look at him again.

Nat's brow was furrowed. "No. I like to watch Alecia when she experiences pleasure." He looked up at his wife and smiled tenderly. "She's so damn pretty, isn't she?" Nat reached out and tucked a strand of her hair behind her ear. "I like to watch her enjoy herself. I like to watch her get lost in the pleasure when I'm not as lost as she is." He looked at Palu with a frown. "Does that make sense?"

"Oh, Natty," she said with a sweet sigh of delight.

Palu's chest constricted at the odd tender moment between husband and wife. "It doesn't make you jealous?" he heard himself ask, and then cursed inwardly. Was he trying to talk them out of what they were doing? He was ten times a fool.

Nat shook his head slightly. "No, I want her to be happy. And I know Alecia loves me."

And not those other men was left unspoken, but Palu understood. This wasn't about him so much as it was about Nat and Alecia. They may want him and find him intriguing right now, but tomorrow he would simply be another man they'd shared, and they'd still be together. Nat threw him into confusion with his next words, however.

"But with you, Palu, I want to watch both of you lost in each other."

"Mmm, yes," Alecia murmured and she leaned forward and brushed her mouth against Palu's. She rubbed her lower lip on his and without thinking he opened to her. When her mouth sank down on his, hot and open and eager, he forgot about words. Alecia's tongue crept into his mouth, as shy as she could sometimes be, and Palu groaned at the taste and sweetness of her. His hands slid up her back to cup the sharp blades of her shoulders as he sat up straighter and pressed her to him. Alecia wrapped her arms around his neck and clung to him as if she was being tossed by stormy seas and needed something to hold on to. He felt the same.

She was delicate and delicious and hungry and his for that moment. He took over the kiss, exploring her mouth with his tongue, drinking her sighs and inhaling her fragrance in deep breaths. Her breasts were mashed against his chest and he felt her hard little nipples and the rapid beating of her heart.

Suddenly Palu felt Nat gently bite the *tatau* on his arm, and Nat's hand sliding around to grip the inside of his thigh. He couldn't control the shudder of desire that racked him. They wanted him.

He ran his hands down Alecia's back and gripped her hips once more. Without breaking the kiss he pressed her down, until the head of his cock found her hot, wet entrance. He backed off and readjusted himself until his cock nestled into her slit, cushioned on her damp, soft hair, his sensitive head bumping into the hard little button hidden there.

Alecia broke the kiss with a cry. "Palu," she exclaimed, her nails digging into his back. They stayed like that for a minute, their panting the only sound in the room.

"Don't worry, Alecia," he said softly into her golden curls, rubbing his nose in her beautiful, lavender-scented hair. "I won't come inside. I'll stay out here."

"More," Nat finally whispered, and he rose up to straddle Palu behind Alecia. He pressed close to her back and placed his hands over Palu's on her hips.

Palu could only think, *yes, like this, together*, as Nat pushed Alecia down onto his cock. Alecia's hips gave a little jerk as his cock was pressed deeper into her creamy heat. Palu watched her bite her lip as her cheeks turned pinker and her eyes glazed. He wanted nothing more than to shove his hips up and cram every dark inch of his cock into her as far as he could go, but he held back. Palu rocked his hips gently and her head fell back on Nat's chest.

"Are you all right?" Palu asked quietly, desperate to move, but just as desperate not to hurt her. He only wanted pleasure for her. There were other ways they could do this, other things they could do to each other.

Alecia laughed weakly. "All right? I'm marvelous. You're so thick, Palu, and so hot against me. It feels delicious," she sighed.

Nat laughed quietly behind her. "He looks as if he'd be delicious inside, too," he commented and Palu couldn't control the rough jerk of his hips. Alecia squeaked and then moaned. "I think she liked that," he told Palu, his voice rough. "Do it again."

"Christ, I want to fuck her so damn *hard*," Palu groaned as he thrust gently up against Alecia again. She ground her cunt down against him, their wet pubic hair mingling and rubbing and Palu hissed in a breath at the exquisite pleasure of it. Her cunt hugged him almost as closely outside as he imagined it would inside. The kiss of the lips of her sex on his cock was robbing him of speech and thought.

Alecia shook her head and groaned as she rubbed back and forth, Palu's cock barely moving up and down her crease with her movements, grinding the head of his cock against her velvet soft lips and hard clitoris. "I can't," she gasped. "I'm sorry, Palu, but I can't."

His cheek was pressed against the side of her head and he rumbled soothingly in her ear. "No, don't be sorry, Alecia. There's nothing to be sorry for."

Alecia bit her lip on a moan. "You're so big." She ground harder against him and they both groaned. "This feels absolutely divine. Please tell me it feels good to you, too."

"It's bloody fucking amazing," he growled, echoing Nat's favorite phrase. As he said it he became aware of Nat behind Alecia, watching them. He looked at the other man and Nat's eyes were narrow, blinding blue slits of desire in a face taut with arousal as he watched Palu and Alecia fuck. Even as Palu thought it, he knew it to be true. He may not be inside her, but this was fucking, this was closer to anyone than he had been in years.

When Nat caught Palu's eye he leaned back to sit on his heels. Then he caught Alecia's bottom in his palms and pressed her up until only the head of Palu's cock was still nestled against her, rising from his crotch as if seeking her. Nat tilted his head far to the side, and then titled his body as well, until he could look under Alecia. Palu knew Nat was looking at his cock, gleaming with Alecia's juices, resting against her creamy, pink cunt.

"Gorgeous," Nat sighed thickly. "Your cock with its black *tatau* up against my wife is absolutely gorgeous, Palu." He pressed Alecia back down and Palu groaned desperately as he was enveloped in her wet heat again. Alecia whimpered.

Nat and Palu both froze. Palu could barely speak through the thickness of desire clogging his throat. "Are you all right?" he rasped, as Nat leaned forward to reach over her shoulder and tenderly brush Alecia's thick, curling hair off her face.

"Lee?" Nat asked quietly. "We can stop."

She shook her head. "No! Please, don't stop. God, it feels so good." She thrust against him, the grinding thrust of before, and Palu thrust back, trying to be gentle. She didn't want gentle. "Fuck me, Palu, hard, the way you want." Her eyes flew open, foggy with desire and she panted softly. "Not fuck. I mean…"

"This?" Palu asked, slipping back and forth in her folds.

"Yes, yes," she cried out, pulling against his hands and Nat's. "Please."

He couldn't deny her and slammed his hips up. She cried out and dug her nails into his shoulders. But she pushed back and slid just as roughly along his length, and Palu grunted at the pleasure.

As he fucked against Alecia, Nat cupped her breasts in his palms and kneaded the pale globes. His touch wasn't gentle, and Palu realized that Alecia was not as delicate as he'd feared. She liked her pleasure a little rough, perhaps. Palu leaned forward and sucked a small, hard, pink nipple into his mouth. Nat pressed her breast high, angling it for Palu. He pulled deeply on her nipple, and then bit down, not too hard, but not soft, either. Alecia screamed, but it sounded odd, and Palu looked up to see her biting her lip to hold back her cries. He smiled around the morsel in his mouth and then sucked the nipple back in, harder than before. Alecia's hands gripped his head, her fingers pulled at his hair, and Palu loved every sharp tug.

It didn't take long before she was on the brink of her release. "Oh God, Palu. God," she groaned. "I'm going to come. I'm sorry, I can't wait. I can't." She cried out the last as she wrapped her arms around his neck again and ground down on his shaft. Palu pulled off her breast with one final tug, and then he felt the contractions of her cunt against his cock as she came. He pressed up, gave her his cock to ride however she wanted it, and let her enjoy her pleasure.

She was so goddamned beautiful as she came. She threw her head back on Nat's shoulder again and keened under her breath. She bit her juicy, red lower lip, and squeezed her eyes shut. Her face turned a bright shade of pink as she continued to moan quietly. Her peak went on and on, and her nails scored his shoulders deeply as he gave short, hard thrusts to her. It was enough to push him over the edge. His cock gave a hard jerk and his release washed over them both, the heat of his sticky semen bathing both of them, soaking their pubic hair and their stomachs. Palu had never felt such pleasure, not just in his own peak but in a lover's. Watching and listening to Alecia's pleasure with Nat watching them both, his hunger and excitement evident in his flushed cheeks and bright blue eyes, was the most erotic thing Palu had ever done. In every way he and Nat had shared the moment with Alecia, shared the pleasure and her body.

When it was over she collapsed atop him, only Nat's arms holding her up.

"Lee?" Palu asked, and then he realized he'd used Nat's special nickname for her. He was afraid he'd trespassed when Nat stared at him intently. He was about to apologize when Nat grinned ferociously.

"My turn," Nat said.

Nat gently lifted Alecia off of Palu's cock and the wet sound they made as they parted caused Nat's cock to jerk and he felt a drop of moisture leak out his slit. Christ they had been beautiful and so god damned arousing, fucking each other that way, hard and gentle at the same time, grinding into one another. And now they were both covered with Palu's seed, the musky scent of their mutual release filling the air and Nat's lungs. He was a little unsteady as the heady perfume swelled his cock to even greater proportions.

"Natty?" Alecia mumbled as she curled into the sheets next to Palu. "Are you going to fuck now?" She sounded so sleepy and satisfied.

Nat brushed her hair out of her eyes. "Yes, angel."

"Oh, good," she sighed. "You're going to enjoy Palu so much." She snuggled up to Palu's hip and kissed it, not even lifting her head from the bed. "He's so beautiful." She languidly lifted her hand and traced the *tatau* on his thigh with a finger. "Isn't he?"

Nat looked at Palu then and caught him gazing at Alecia with so much longing that it made Nat ache to see it. "Yes," Nat agreed quietly, "he is beautiful."

Palu's eyes jerked over to Nat, and he blushed. Nat laughed. "Have I embarrassed you?" he asked with a teasing grin.

Palu nodded once, stiffly. "Men are not beautiful."

Alecia laughed gaily, clearly regaining her equilibrium. "Oh, silly, silly Palu," she said, tapping his thigh. "Trust me when I tell you that you are most definitely beautiful."

"I've never seen anything as beautiful as the two of you fucking," Nat told him roughly, his breathing unsteady. "The sight of that cock sliding through my wife's cunt, her pale arms wrapped around you, so white against the black of your *tatau*. Your release spilling all over her."

Palu was breathing just as roughly. "Fuck me," he growled. "I want to be inside you, Nat."

"Oh, yes," Alecia moaned. "Please fuck him for me, Natty. Please."

Nat laughed, thrilled at how much they both wanted this. "Tell me what you want me to do," he ordered Palu, hunger gnawing at him as he stared at Palu's cock, which was already growing hard again.

Palu sat back against the head of the bed again and soundlessly motioned Nat over. Nat straddled Palu's legs again and he lowered himself until one of Palu's muscled thighs pressed against the crease between his buttocks. Palu growled wordlessly and Nat shivered at the sound.

"I want to fuck you," Palu told him roughly, leaning forward and grabbing Nat by the back of the neck. Palu fell back against the wooden headboard and pulled Nat with him. Nat fell on him, his hands pressed to Palu's chest. Nat couldn't believe how big and hard his pectoral muscles were. He slid his hands over until he covered Palu's hard little nipples and he ground his palms against them. This time Palu bared his teeth in a feral smile before yanking Nat's mouth to his.

Nat had been fantasizing about kissing Palu since he'd first seen him in the ballroom earlier. The fantasy was tame compared to the thrill of feeling Palu's warm, soft lips on his. Nat opened wide and invited Palu inside his mouth, and Palu answered the invitation, his tongue venturing boldly in to search out all Nat's secrets. Nat met each of Palu's bold forays with matching fervor. Palu tasted hot and needy, a heady combination. Nat inhaled and almost lost what little composure he had left when he smelled Alecia on Palu. Their combined scents drove him higher against Palu, and he awkwardly walked his knees forward without breaking the kiss. When their cocks touched they both groaned and Nat slid his hands up Palu's chest to cup Palu's jaw. He ran his thumbs over Palu's cheekbones, and then pushed his hands into Palu's wildly curling hair. He pressed against Palu, until his stomach was coated in the semen that still covered Palu's stomach.

Palu groaned and rubbed his cock against Nat's. Nat pulled away from the kiss with a gasp, and Palu immediately began to kiss his neck and jaw. Palu's cock was a hot, slick brand against his, wet with Alecia's cream, Palu's release and the moisture that was leaking from Palu.

"Now," Nat gasped, "I need you now."

Palu shook his head. "I'm too big, Nat. Let me ready you first."

Nat rested his forehead on Palu's with a weak laugh. "Christ, I forgot about that. Yes, please."

"Here," Alecia murmured. Nat looked down to see her roll over and run a finger through the semen on Palu's stomach. Nat could smell their release all around them, and it smelled so bloody good he groaned.

Suddenly Palu's hand reached out and he thrust a finger into Alecia's cunt. "Give me some of yours," he growled and Alecia moaned and scooted closer. "Yes," she said, "take it."

And then Nat knew what they were about. Palu was getting his finger wet so he could stretch Nat with it, with Alecia's moisture coating it.

"Oh God," Nat groaned, and then Palu's finger was there, pressing inside his hole. Nat hissed at the burn of the initial invasion, but Palu went slow, his finger gently swirling in exploration, testing Nat's boundaries. Nat relaxed, and Palu's finger slid further inside.

"That's right, Natty," Palu whispered in his ear, "let me in. You're so hot and tight here, Nat. How many men have been here?"

Nat laughed breathlessly and then moaned as Palu fucked his finger out and back in. "Not enough to prepare me for you," he said in a shaky voice.

Palu grabbed a handful of Nat's arse and shoved his finger in deep. Nat cried out, but there was only pleasure, no pain. "Answer me," Palu growled.

"Not many, Palu," Alecia told him quietly, "not in the last few years." She rose up to straddle Palu's legs behind Nat. She mirrored their earlier positions exactly, except their roles were reversed. "Nat likes to fuck better than being fucked." Alecia ran her hands soothingly over Nat's shoulders and down his arms. "Don't you, Nat?"

"Yes," he ground out as Palu found his sweet spot and tapped his finger against it. Nat shuddered.

"Why are you letting me fuck you?" Palu asked quietly. Nat opened his eyes. He hadn't even realized he'd closed them. Palu was watching him intently.

"Because this is what I wanted from the second I saw you," Nat told him, unable to lie. "I wanted to feel you inside me."

Palu growled again and buried his face in Nat's neck, kissing him. "That doesn't mean I don't plan on fucking you, too," Nat told him thickly, pressing down on Palu's thick, rough finger deep inside him. "I want to fuck into your *tatau*."

Palu chuckled against his skin, and Nat felt gooseflesh erupt on his arms. "Just as you want Palu's *tatau* fucking into your pretty, white arse," Palu told him roughly.

"God, yes," he said weakly. He was trembling at Palu's words, and the picture he painted. "Now, please."

Palu pulled his finger out slowly and Nat's breath hitched in his chest. Palu licked Nat's neck and then nipped his jaw. "I need more than what Alecia can give us." Palu rubbed his finger across his stomach, gathering the creamy fluid, and then he pressed back inside. "Not enough," he murmured. "My cock will need more."

"Lee," Nat said, barely able to think much less speak at this point. Bloody hell, Palu was going to fuck him. Right now his finger was coated with his seed and he was fucking Nat with it. Nat shivered.

Nat rubbed his face against Palu's hair as he heard the bed linens rustling and a drawer open. He tried to ignore the sounds. He wanted to stay where he was, full of the magic of Palu. Palu's hair was coarse, but not rough. It tickled his cheeks, and smelled like soap, so clean and marvelous, and sexual musk, an aphrodisiac like no other. Nat pulled back a bit when Palu pushed him gently away. Palu pulled his finger out and Nat ached with desire there.

"Help me," Palu whispered thickly to Alecia as she poured oil into his hand. She poured some into her hand and then capped the bottle. When both of their hands wrapped around his cock and began to massage the oil in Palu groaned and Nat's back passage trembled.

As Palu and Alecia rubbed the oil on his cock, Nat fingered the gray hairs at Palu's temple. "How old are you?" he asked, running his fingers through that hair, extracting them gently when they got tangled in Palu's curls.

"Thirty-six," Palu replied. He grabbed Nat's hips and pulled him back in. "Look at me, Nat."

Nat looked down, and he could see the candle flame from across the room reflected in Palu's dark eyes.

"How do you want this, Nat?" Palu asked. "I think it would be easier if you were on your knees."

"Mmm," Alecia hummed behind him. "Yes. So I can see."

That was enough to pull Nat out of his strange stupor. Suddenly lust slammed into him so hard he lost his balance and had to steady himself with a hand on Palu's hard, sticky stomach. "Yes, so Alecia can watch," he growled. "Yes, that's what I want."

Alecia scrambled off Palu's legs and Palu pushed Nat off him and down on the mattress. "On your knees, Natty," Palu growled. "I can't wait much longer. You two have me about to spend right now, and I'm not even inside you yet."

"Don't you fucking dare," Nat growled over his shoulder at him as he pushed up on his knees, "not until you're inside."

Palu grinned darkly back. "You don't tell me what to do, Nat. Not now."

"The hell I don't," Nat snarled. He was wild for this dark stranger.

Suddenly Alecia was there, her hand fisted in Nat's hair. "Bad Natty," she whispered. She leaned in and bit his lip sharply, and Nat jerked back. Alecia laughed. "Settle down, darling. Palu wants to fuck you." Alecia ran her hand softly over Nat's hair. "You look so good, Nat. I love to watch you. I love to watch you and Palu."

Nat leaned forward and kissed her, waiting. But Palu simply sat on his knees behind Nat, not touching him. Nat broke the kiss and looked over his shoulder to see Palu staring at Alecia.

"Come," he said to her and held out his hand. Alecia crawled to his side and Palu bent to kiss the corner of her mouth, then her cheek, and finally his lips came to rest on her ear. "Help me," he said again. He reached for the oil and poured some drops in Nat's crease. Palu caught the oil on his fingers and rubbed it around Nat's entrance. It felt so good and Nat bit his lip to hold back another moan. Once Alecia put the bottle down Palu guided Alecia's oil-slick hand to Nat's behind. Palu pressed his finger back in and Nat gasped, his head dropping forward. Suddenly he felt another touch and a second, smaller finger pressed inside.

"Oh God," Alecia whispered, and Nat couldn't control his shaking. Christ, Alecia had her finger inside him.

"Have you ever done this?" Palu whispered. "Have you ever fucked your husband like this, Alecia?" Another finger was added, slick and smooth, Alecia's, and Nat groaned.

"No," she whispered. "He's so tight and hot."

"Mmm," Palu hummed, the sound deep and aroused. "Yes, he is." Then Palu pressed another finger inside. Nat was on fire, but it was a sweet, wild burn.

"You can take these fingers, Nat," Palu told him with satisfaction. "Should we fuck you now?"

"Right fucking now," Nat gasped and Palu laughed before they both slid their fingers out.

"Watch," Palu told him, tugging his hip. Nat looked over his shoulder and saw Alecia's hand guiding Palu's cock to his hole. Christ, the *tatau* was bloody beautiful.

Palu pressed his cock against Nat's entrance and Nat held his breath. Then Palu was inside, so big and thick that Nat feared he couldn't take him, couldn't take that beautiful cock with its dark *tataus*.

"Breathe, Nat," Palu whispered, "breathe and relax. Let me in."

"Oh, Nat," Alecia breathed, "it's perfect, absolutely perfect."

"Ah, kiss me, Alecia," Palu purred, and Nat felt her weight settle on her hands against his buttocks as she complied. When they broke the kiss Nat could hear both of them breathing heavily over his back, and he knew without a doubt that this was the most exciting thing he and Alecia had ever done.

Nat forced his back out of its instinctive bow and made the muscles clenched tight around Palu's cock relax, too. Alecia moved to sit on her heels in front of him. Nat pressed his face to the bed linens between her knees. Suddenly Palu thrust all the way into him, and Nat had no time to tense against him. He was panting, his arse on fire.

"Nat?" Alecia asked. "Are you all right?"

"Christ, it feels like he split me in two," he whispered.

Palu was rubbing his hands over Nat's back and buttocks. "I'm sorry, Nat," he said quietly, and Nat could hear the sincerity in his voice. "Do you want me to pull out?"

"No," Nat told him quickly. "No, just let me get used to it." He took several deep breaths and concentrated on Palu's hands rubbing his backside, and then Alecia began to knead his shoulders and smooth her hands gently over his upper back. It was so soothing, so relaxing, and soon Nat found that the fullness in his back passage was pleasurable instead of painful, the heat there of a different kind.

Nat snaked his arms up around Alecia's thighs and grabbed her sweet, plump bottom in both palms. She squeaked and Nat chuckled. Palu's warm rumble of a laugh made gooseflesh skitter up his back and Nat jerked a little at the sensation. His movement caused Palu's cock to move within him, hitting him deep, and Nat moaned.

"Oh, that sounded good," Alecia murmured.

"Yes, it did," Palu agreed in that deep, rich voice, and one hand slid down to grasp Nat's hip while the other stayed on his lower back, pressing him down to hold him in place. "Nat?"

Nat knew what he was asking. "Yes," he said, his voice thick. Alecia rose up on her knees again so that Nat had to let go of her bottom and instead held onto her legs. Her hands slid down his back until they were right above Palu's. "Have you got a good view?" Nat asked with amused indulgence.

"Mmm, yes," she hummed happily, and Palu laughed again. Then he tentatively pulled out, just an inch or two, and pressed back in.

"Bloody hell," Nat cried out, arching his back. It was the most incredible thing he'd ever felt. No one had ever felt like this inside him, no one.

Palu froze.

"No," Nat said, his breathing ragged. "I meant bloody hell that feels amazing."

"Ah," Palu chuckled roughly, "bloody fucking amazing."

Nat laughed breathlessly. "Exactly."

"Then I won't stop," Palu told him, and he did it again. And again.

Nat lost track of time. He just lay there holding tight to Alecia while Palu showed him what this was supposed to be between men.

He could hear Alecia above him, her breathing ragged as every now and then a moan escaped. Christ, she loved to watch him with another man. He was fiercely glad, glad that something he enjoyed so much also brought her pleasure. Her nails dug into his back, and it was just one more layer of sensation on top of the incredible things Palu was doing to Nat with that primitive-looking cock of his.

"Nat," Palu groaned. His hands slid up Nat's back and Alecia pulled back. Palu's hands continued down his arms to hold Nat's hands over Alecia's calves. The heat and hardness of Palu's chest pressed him down and he buried his face against Nat's nape. "I can't wait, Natty. I'm going to come inside you," he groaned. "Come with me." Palu pushed a hand under Nat and wrapped his big fist around Nat's aching cock and Nat shouted at the streak of heat that raced from cock to balls to buttocks.

"God," Palu said roughly in his ear as he worked Nat's cock and fucked him with controlled force. "It's been a very long time since I watched this dark cock of mine with its black *tatau* fuck a sweet, tight, white arse. It looks so damn good. *You* look so damn good, Natty, taking it so hot and tight. And the little sounds you make..."

Nat was momentarily startled. He made little sounds?

Palu's grip on his cock tightened then and Nat knew he was going to come. His balls pulled up and tingled, and he felt the pressure, the ache of his impending release.

"Nat," Palu cried out, and his fist squeezed tight as he pressed deep into Nat and came. Palu's hips jerked shallowly inside him and Nat could feel the slick heat of his seed. It was enough. With a shout he came, his cock pumping hard in Palu's fist.

Palu collapsed above him, but he still supported most of his weight on his arms so Nat didn't feel crushed. He should have. He should have felt suffocated beneath the larger man, by his physical weight and the weight of what he'd made Nat feel as he fucked him into oblivion. But he didn't. All he felt was content.

Alecia still kneeled in front of them. She leaned back, and Nat lifted his head just a little to see her knees spread, the fingers of one hand tunneling into her cunt while she rubbed her clitoris with the other. He could still see Palu's earlier release on her.

Nat moved until he was next to Alecia and he tugged on her leg. "Open up, Lee," he whispered. "I want to see what Palu tastes like."

Alecia complied readily, turning onto her back and spreading her legs. Nat leaned down and buried his nose in her wet hair. It smelled sharp and tangy, like the ocean. Did he smell like that now? He felt the slick heat of Palu's seed trickling down his crease and moaned. He pulled back and slid the tip of his tongue into her slit. The combination of Palu and

Alecia there was ambrosia. Nat groaned and began to lick her stomach clean.

"Mmm," Palu growled. He came to his knees and kissed Nat on the back. "What do I taste like?" he murmured.

"Like the ocean," Nat told him, nibbling on Alecia's stomach, sucking Palu's seed off her soft skin. "Like adventure, and discovery, and excitement."

Palu's laugh rumbled along Nat's nerve endings, leaving gooseflesh behind. "All that? I had no idea I was so tasty. Let me see." He leaned down over Alecia, and tangled his tongue with Nat's as he licked her clean. Alecia moaned and thrust her hips up.

"My quim, Nat," she said breathlessly. "Lick me there. Both of you."

Nat pressed his mouth against her sex and thrust his tongue between her folds, licking the hidden valleys there, finding the tangy taste he craved. Alecia moaned and thrust again, and then Nat felt Palu's breath on his ear, and he heard Palu sucking on the hard button at the apex of her slit. She cried out and her legs fell open further. Her hand pressed against Nat's head, holding his mouth on her, and he fought her grip until he could lift his head enough to see her other hand buried in Palu's curls, holding him on that spot he was sucking and licking with abandon.

In moments she was bucking beneath them, crying out with another release. Nat pressed a finger inside her, into that space that had been his and his alone for years now, and something made him grab Palu's hand and bring it there, made him press Palu's finger in beside his until they both filled her. Alecia sobbed her pleasure as she gripped the fingers inside her, her strong contractions pressing their two fingers together.

When Alecia's muscles relaxed, Nat sat up. Palu was staring at their two hands pressed so tightly to her, their two fingers clearly fucking into her. Nat's breathing was ragged.

He'd never shared Alecia like this, never. His heart was pounding with excitement, but also fear. Why tonight? Why Palu?

Alecia gave a breathless laugh. "Oh, Natty," she sighed. And didn't that just say it all?

Chapter Five

&

Alecia was in heaven. They had bathed, and she was snuggled on Nat's lap at the head of the bed, her feet resting on Palu's beautiful thigh. She frowned. He was too far away.

"Come closer," she ordered, pouting. She grabbed Palu's arm and tugged, pulling him closer to Nat until the two men's shoulders were touching. She liked the look of that, of Nat's broad shoulder with those darling freckles next to Palu's wide, heavily muscled one, with the black, curling primitive swirls of ink in his skin. Palu ran his hand up Alecia's leg, kneading her calf and the back of her thigh and Alecia sighed with contentment.

"That feels wonderful," she said happily, smoothing her hand over the light dusting of hair on Nat's chest. His nipples peaked and Alecia ran a finger around one of them, toying with it.

"Lee," Nat laughed, brushing her hand away. He shivered a little, and she rubbed his arm briskly. "I'm just a little too sensitive still, I think."

"Are you all right?" Palu asked again. He was so sweet, so worried about Nat, afraid he'd been too rough. But Nat had loved it, Alecia could tell. And Nat had reassured them both of that repeatedly.

"Palu, for the last time I am fine. I am better than fine. I am well-fucked and content to be so. Please stop asking me. You'd think you'd never fucked a man before." Nat went still beneath her and looked at Palu with wide eyes. "You have fucked a man before, haven't you?"

Palu laughed, shaking the bed. "Many. I don't think I need to tell you that women are few and far between on a ship sailing in uncharted and dangerous waters."

"Was it common then, for the men on board to fuck one another?" Alecia asked with interest. She rather thought she'd enjoy a ship like that.

Palu raised an eyebrow at her with a little grin. "Indeed no, at least not openly. But liaisons do occur."

"How on earth did you stand it, Palu?" she asked with a shudder. "You must have gone months without."

Palu raised his hands in front of him and turned them several times, examining them. "At one point I was so in love I almost asked my right hand to marry me." Nat snorted with laughter. Palu raised that eyebrow again and added somberly, "But I didn't want my left to get jealous."

Alecia was amused and charmed right down to her toes. He had a sense of humor, too.

"Nat has read everything you've ever written," she told Palu impulsively.

Nat jerked beneath her and grabbed her hand on his chest. When she looked at him he was frowning fiercely at her.

Palu didn't move, but Alecia felt his withdrawal anyway. "Have you?" he asked politely.

What on earth? She had no idea what had prompted his reaction. "Yes, he has. He longs to travel as you do, but we simply do not have the means."

Palu looked at her strangely. "Indeed," was all he said.

Nat cleared his throat. "Well, I'm certainly no scholar, not like you, Palu. An amateur naturalist at most." He glared at Alecia. "And Alecia has read almost as much as I have."

Alecia blushed. "Only because I wanted to be able to understand what you were talking about," she rushed to explain. "And I still don't understand but half of it." She desperately hoped Palu wouldn't want to discuss his research.

She had been feeling so happy and content, she had no wish to ruin it by showing how ignorant she was. Why did she bring it up? Why?

"Don't be ridiculous, Alecia," Nat snapped. "You are quite intelligent, and uphold your end of any conversation."

Alecia glowed with happiness at his praise. When they'd married she'd been a silly little eighteen-year-old girl who knew nothing but ball gowns and gossip. How Nat had intimidated her! But he'd encouraged her to spread her wings and he'd shown her a whole new world with his studies.

"You both must have been very happy to find me, then," Palu said in that cool, polite voice. Alecia did not like that voice.

"Imagine our surprise when we realized that you were *the* Gregory Anderson," Nat said cautiously. "We had no idea you were back in England, much less at Wilchester's."

Palu was looking so intently at them that Alecia squirmed. His hand tightened on her leg, but he didn't seem aware of it. "Not many people knew I was back," he said, his tone not quite so chilly.

Alecia laughed nervously. "Honestly, Palu, I had no idea that the writer of those dry scientific treatises would be so handsome and arresting."

Palu smiled reluctantly and Alecia realized what she'd said. She bit her lip in horror.

"Yes, very nice, Alecia," Nat drawled. "Tell the man who just took us both past the edge of reason that he's boring. Well done."

At that Palu laughed and relaxed. "So you didn't know who I was when you approached me?"

Alecia suddenly understood. "Oh, Palu. Do a great many people approach you because of who you are?"

He nodded and began kneading her leg again, refusing to look at her. "It is quite a coup to bed Gregory Anderson, scholar and curiosity."

"Curiosity?" Nat asked quietly. He put his hand on Palu's, stilling his movements.

Palu's hand tightened around Alecia's leg again. "Do you know many other Englishmen who look as I do? Whose mothers were natives?"

"No." Nat pried Palu's hand off of her and brought it to his mouth, kissing his palm. Palu watched with those deep, dark, secretive eyes. "Which makes you unique, not a curiosity."

Palu snorted. "They are one and the same."

Nat tipped his head as he stared back at Palu. "You write about the plants and animals you discover on your journeys, but not the people. Your father became famous writing about the people."

Palu frowned. "They are my people. I will not turn them into specimens to be pinned to a board and studied." He looked away for a moment, and then he spun about to face them again. "My father loved me, you know."

Alecia couldn't stand the hurt in his voice. She reached for him, clutching his arm. "Of course he did, Palu. He was your father."

Now it was Nat's turn to snort. "You of all people know that means nothing, Alecia."

It hurt. But Nat was correct. Her father barely tolerated her. He'd married her off to Nat to gain a connection into the upper classes. Instead he got a daughter and son-in-law who skirted the edge of polite society with their unusual interests and sexual appetites. And to top off her failure as a daughter, she'd failed to produce a grandchild to assure the connection was permanently established.

Nat hugged her hard. "I'm sorry, Lee," he whispered.

"What do you mean?" Palu asked sharply.

Alecia looked at him and she suddenly wanted to be held in his arms. She wanted all that strength and heat and *tatau* wrapped around her. She surprised Nat when she scampered out of his lap. He gave a yelp as her knee slipped down into his crotch.

"Oh, Nat," she cried out, trying to turn around and move her knee without falling. "Are you all right?"

Nat groaned and cupped his sex. "I wish everyone would stop asking me that," he said breathlessly. He poked at himself experimentally. "I believe we shall live to fight another day."

Palu laughed and settled Alecia in his lap, hugging her tight. "Does your father not appreciate you, pretty Alecia?"

Alecia put her head on his shoulder and hugged him back. Surely it was wrong that he made everything seem all right. "My father dislikes the very sight of me," she told him. "And I believe he wishes he could shoot Nat on sight."

Nat laughed and leaned over to kiss her shoulder. "Too true, my dear."

Palu rested his chin on the top of Alecia's head as Nat rubbed his nose on Palu's shoulder.

"Why do you do it?" he asked quietly.

Alecia was confused, but Nat understood his question. "I didn't know how to love her."

"What?" Alecia said, not sure she'd heard him correctly.

Nat looked at her, settling his shoulder against Palu's. "When we married, I'd never been with a woman before. She was completely innocent, and I might as well have been. Neither one of us enjoyed our time in bed."

Alecia felt her jaw drop. "You'd never been with a woman?" she asked incredulously. "Natty, you never told me that."

He looked surprised. "Haven't I? Well, I suppose I thought it was obvious." He ran his finger down her arm until he took her hand in his. "I blamed her, because I was young and ignorant. I went back to what I knew and enjoyed."

"Men?" Palu asked, his tone curious.

Nat nodded and then grinned at Palu. "I like to fuck men. Just because I got married didn't change that." He shrugged. "And I don't need to tell you that it is easier to find a man to fuck in England than a woman. We are not so heavily guarded."

"That is true," Palu chuckled. "Unless one is lucky enough to find both." He leaned over and kissed Nat while he slid his hand up and fondled Alecia's breast. She held her breath at the sight of the two men kissing, their tongues languidly dueling. She felt her sex open and grow moist, and noticed Palu's cock growing hard beneath her. Nat thrust his hips against Palu's side, and she knew he was getting aroused again, too.

When Palu broke the kiss he smiled tenderly at Nat, and Alecia realized that she'd never seen Nat like this with another man. Nat and Alecia fucked them, one or two had spent the night, and then they left and Nat and Alecia would talk about what they did, but not who. But it was so different with Palu. Everything was different.

"How old are you, pretty Nat?" Palu whispered. Then he turned to look at Alecia, and he leaned down and kissed her nipple. "And innocent Alecia." He sat up and leaned back against the wall. "Just how long have you been married?"

Alecia's breathing was uneven. Such a small, simple thing, a kiss—one for Nat and one for Alecia. And yet she was more aroused by Palu's simple kisses than by the elaborate sexual games played by most of the men they'd entertained here. "We've been married for seven years," she told him. "I'm twenty-five."

Palu looked surprised. "So old, then? I'd thought you younger."

Alecia blushed. "Am I too old for you?" she teased. "You are, after all, an old man of thirty-six." Suddenly she was nervous. She knew older men who wanted their women very young.

Palu grinned wolfishly. "Hardly. You are, I think, perfect."

Nat chuckled and kissed Palu's neck. "Yes, she is." He pulled back with a sigh and sat up. Alecia could see his cock, semi-hard, pink, his sac peeking through his pubic hair beneath. She liked Nat like that, knowing that it would take only a touch, or a kiss, to make him fully erect. The anticipation was delicious. "I'm twenty-six." He ran a hand through his hair, mussing it further. "We were married very young." He shook his head. "Too young."

"But somehow you went from two young, inexperienced, estranged spouses to this," Palu said, and it was more of a question than a statement.

Alecia laughed, surprised at the bitterness in it. Was she still bitter? She'd thought not. "Nat went back to his men and I thought I'd see what he found so wonderful about them," she said crisply. "The first few years of our marriage were not happy ones."

Nat's look was full of pain and regret. Hadn't she made him suffer enough? Hadn't she set out to hurt him, too?

"I'm sorry, Natty," she whispered. She looked away from both men, sitting up in Palu's lap, clasping her hands together. "I adored him, you see, and I knew I was not the ideal wife to him. I was ignorant of everything, not just sexual relations. I was childish and spoiled and I pushed him away because I didn't think I deserved him."

Palu was rubbing her back and she looked over to see Nat staring down at his lap.

"And then?" Palu asked gently.

Alecia smiled, and Nat looked up at her and gave her a little half-smile. "And then there was Simon," she said.

"Simon? Simon Gantry?" Palu asked.

Alecia nodded. "Yes. Simon became lover to us both at the same time. After a while, he suggested that we all three," she waved her hand around, "you know, together."

Nat laughed and waved his hand in imitation of her. "Yes, together." He let his hand drop. "Simon taught us how to love one another. It was pretty simple, actually. We discovered we had a great deal more in common than Simon. After a few months, Simon faded away as he is wont to do, and Alecia and I found that we had fallen in love. With each other." He laughed his sweet, teasing laugh, and Alecia's heart was light again. "Falling in love with your wife. How odd!"

"How odd, indeed," she agreed with a laugh. "But I confess that even though he hurt me, and I him, I never stopped loving him."

"Lee," Nat whispered. He leaned over and kissed her. When his lips touched hers she realized that they had not kissed all night. They had been so intent on Palu. Her heart beat fast and she felt panic. Was it happening again? Were they drifting apart? Was that why she felt so drawn to Palu? But Nat's kiss aroused her as it always did, his taste so familiar and yet so enticing for its very familiarity. She cupped his cheek in her palm as she bit his lower lip. Nat rose to his knees before her and ran his palms from her knees to her thighs, and she quivered at his touch. She could feel Palu watching them, and it heightened her arousal. They'd never shared this with another. They might fuck someone else in their bed, but they only came together when they were private. But suddenly she wanted to do everything for Palu. She wanted to fuck Nat for Palu, for she could tell he enjoyed watching them together. He was breathing heavily, and his hand rested on her backside, kneading it suggestively.

Nat broke the kiss and stared into Alecia's eyes for the longest time. Finally he spoke. "Palu," he said quietly, "would you like to watch me fuck my wife?"

Alecia's heart skipped a beat and she smiled at Nat.

"Yes," Palu answered simply. "Yes, I would."

Palu had never truly seen anything like it before. He'd thought he had. In the islands crew members had not always been circumspect when it came to their sexual encounters. But it was clear that there was a world of difference between what he'd seen and this act born out of love. It was…breathtaking.

Nat lay atop Alecia, slowly thrusting into her, her arms held over her head by Nat's hands in hers. She had her legs wrapped around him, hugging him tight with her heels pressed to his muscular arse. Palu loved the way those muscles flexed in the candlelight as he fucked his gorgeous wife. And Alecia, she had her eyes closed and her perfect, white teeth were clasped on her lower lip. With each thrust her neck arched just a little. The act was simple as they were doing it, but incredibly intimate in its simplicity.

"Lee," Nat whispered, his mouth pressed to her ear. She turned her head on the mattress toward Palu, and opened her eyes. Their eyes met and held, and Alecia smiled. Almost as soon as she released her hold on her lip she moaned as Nat ground into her.

"Natty," she groaned. "Harder."

Palu was mesmerized. They were gorgeous. He couldn't believe he'd fucked them. Did Nat still feel his semen in his passage? Was Alecia still sore from his cock? The thought of them still feeling what Palu had done to them while they fucked one another was exciting beyond belief.

"I love fucking you," Nat whispered. "You're so sweet and wet, Lee, so beautiful."

"Yes," Palu whispered, and then he could have bitten his tongue off, afraid he'd ruined the moment for them.

But instead of resenting his intrusion, Nat turned to him with a teasing smile. "You know, don't you, Palu? You know how sweet her cunt is."

"Nat," Palu groaned. He slid down to lay on his stomach next to them, his cheek resting on his fist as he watched them. He thrust his aching cock into the bed and found a small

70

measure of relief. "You two are perfect." The sounds of their fucking were as arousing as the sight. Alecia's little moans that she tried to stifle—why did she do that? And Nat's heavy breathing and his murmured love words. And she was so wet Palu could hear it every time Nat thrust in and out.

"Palu," Alecia moaned. She tugged her hand free from Nat's grip and reached for him. Palu took her hand and kissed it. "Come, Palu," she whispered.

Palu grinned. "Yes, I think I will, just from watching you."

Nat groaned and Alecia laughed breathlessly. "No, silly," she said, pulling on his hand. "Come over here and let us taste you again."

Palu groaned, but shook his head. "No, this is about you and Nat."

Nat looked at him with a frown. "No, it's about you too, Palu. It's been about you since we first saw you. Don't you know that?"

He wanted to believe Nat. He wanted to believe that these two young lovers wanted to share this moment with him. No matter how foolish or ridiculous that might be, he wanted to believe it. Rising to his knees he moved until he kneeled beside Alecia's head on the mattress. He lowered his hands to the bed on the other side of them, so that he was leaning over them, his cock above Alecia, in front of Nat. The sight of his hard cock hanging there framed by their flushed faces made him want to howl in satisfaction. He took several deep breaths, trying to calm down.

Then Nat tentatively licked Palu's cock with the tip of his tongue, and Palu came undone. He began to shake and fisted his hands in the bed linens so tightly he thought he might rip them. He lowered his hips slowly, and Alecia opened her mouth to suckle the head of his cock. Palu bit his lip and forced himself to hold still for them. Nat traced his *tatau* with his tongue again, as he'd done earlier. Palu had never been so glad he'd gotten them as he was tonight.

"You're shaking," Nat whispered. "Because of us?"

"Yes." He couldn't speak anymore. He didn't want to speak. He didn't want to reveal the tumult of emotions drowning him.

Nat stopped licking him, and Palu was both glad and devastated. Alecia's lips were still wrapped around him, but she was being very gentle with him, as if she knew he was at the breaking point. Nat began to thrust harder into Alecia and her head moved on the bed and against his cock. He couldn't hold back his groan.

"Yes," Nat growled, his pace increasing. And then Alecia was crying out around Palu's cock, her legs locked around Nat, her back arching. Palu pulled back from the exquisite sensation of her voice vibrating down his shaft. He sat on his heels and watched Alecia's face as she came. And then he saw the tremors in Nat's back, the bunched muscles of his buttocks, and Nat buried his face in Alecia's neck as he came with a whimper, the same whimper he'd made when Palu had fucked him. That Nat should make the same noise for him and Alecia made him inordinately pleased.

When they were both done, lying there panting, Palu assumed they were spent. But suddenly Nat rose onto his hands and knees and turned to him. Without a word he grabbed Palu's cock in one hand and then he sucked it deep into his mouth. Palu shouted out wordlessly and thrust into the wet heat of his mouth. Nat growled and tugged on Palu's hip to turn him slightly. As soon as the angle was right Nat began to fuck Palu with his mouth, sucking hard on each fast stroke up and then sliding down slowly. Saliva ran down Palu's shaft from Nat's mouth, coating his testicles, as Nat hummed his pleasure at his taste and swirled his tongue over the tip. Palu grabbed Nat's hair in one big fist and started moving his head at a faster pace. He'd needed this, so badly.

How had Nat known? He could never fuck Alecia like this, she was too small. But Nat's mouth was made to be fucked by him.

"I'm going to come, Nat," he growled, hoping against hope that Nat didn't pull away. He wanted to fill Nat's mouth, fill Nat. He wanted someone to take his release inside them and not throw it away. Nat wouldn't throw it away. Nat hadn't thrown it away.

Nat grabbed his thigh and tugged Palu closer, sucking him down into his throat. Palu groaned as he came, trying to watch Nat the whole time, not wanting to miss Nat taking him like this.

When it was over Nat twisted his head out of Palu's grip and pulled off his cock with a gasp. He was laughing. "I've never been mouth-fucked so well before," he said, his voice rough, as if his throat hurt. Palu felt a primitive thrill that he'd used Nat that way and put the gravel in his voice. Alecia laughed and shimmied up to kiss Nat, still laughing. Then she turned to Palu and kissed him, too, with the taste of him and Nat still on her smiling lips.

Palu felt the ground shifting beneath him. He wanted more than one night with these two. They made him long for things he'd given up hope of ever having. And that was dangerous. He knew it, but he couldn't stop the tide of longing that pulled him ever closer to them.

Chapter Six

ဆ

Palu walked into the drawing room and Nat turned from where he was standing at the window. He had one hand braced against the frame and he'd been looking out on the street with a frown. He wiped the expression from his face but not before he saw Palu make note of it.

"All cleaned up?" he asked lightly, moving away from the window.

"Yes, thank you," Palu replied politely. Nat had noticed that the other man retreated into painstaking politeness when he was unsure of a situation. The refuge of the well-bred Englishman, Nat thought wryly.

"Where is Alecia?" Nat asked, ignoring Palu's questioning look.

Palu gave him a genuine, amused smile. "She evicted me from her dressing room. She said I took up too much space and distracted her with my intense observation of her toiletry."

Nat laughed. "Don't worry. I have received much the same treatment on occasion."

Nat didn't know what to do. Should he walk back over to the window and pretend occupation with the busy street? Or should he sit down and pretend a nonchalance he didn't feel? He stood there staring at Palu in indecision and frustration.

"Tell me what is wrong, Nat," Palu demanded quietly. "Do you wish me to leave?"

"Leave?" Nat's astonishment was genuine. "No! Do you wish to leave?" He couldn't leave yet. It was too soon.

Palu shook his head. "No. But your behavior seems agitated. Why?"

Nat chose the option of sitting. He dropped onto the settee and clasped his hands together, his elbows on his knees. He couldn't look at Palu. "Agitated behavior? Are you going to write a study of me?"

"No one would believe the things I've seen you do."

Nat barked with laughter and looked up to see Palu giving him a barely-there, wry grin. "Yes, well, I am a nimble fellow, aren't I?" Nat felt himself blushing. The things they had done over the last day and two nights were almost unbelievable to Nat as well. Had he really let this man fuck him over and over, shared his wife, licked, nibbled, sucked and tasted every inch of Palu's dark, *tataued* skin? Yes, he had. And he'd do it again. He was hoping to do it again, at least.

"What do you study?" Palu asked suddenly. Nat jerked his head in surprise. Palu had an intent look on his face, watching Nat closely. "I know you have read my work, but you have not talked about your interests."

Nat blushed. "My interests are not as broad as yours." He cleared his throat self-consciously. "Fish." At Palu's blank look he expanded his answer. "I'm interested in fish. Your father's writings mention a few of the new species he saw in the South Seas. But yours do not. Do you know anything of the fish there?"

Palu smiled engagingly. "Only the ones that are good to eat."

Nat sighed. He'd hoped the topic would occupy them for a while.

"They are beautiful." Palu's comment brought Nat's head up again. He looked for signs of mockery or indulgence, but Palu actually seemed interested in the discussion. "There are many that are similar to those found here in Europe, but there are also many fish that are breathtakingly beautiful, masterpieces of color and design and form. They are quite exotic, and in some cases quite lethal."

"Lethal?" Nat sat forward, fascinated.

Palu nodded. "Yes, as in poisonous. So when I say I know which ones are good to eat, I meant more than mere taste." His smile was amused and brought out the dimples in his cheeks. He was so bloody fucking gorgeous that Nat wanted to jump across the room and take him right there.

He stood up, not caring that his restlessness confirmed his agitation. He paced over to the bookcase along the wall. "You make Alecia very happy," he told Palu honestly. He spun to face the other man who still stood where he'd stopped when he came in the room. He caught surprise and relief on Palu's face. "Thank you."

"You thank me?" Palu asked incredulously. He finally walked across the room, not stopping until he was roughly a foot away from Nat. "Nat, this time with you and Alecia has been one of the single most enjoyable things I've ever experienced. I thank you for letting me be with you."

Nat shook his head, denying Palu's gratitude. "No. You don't understand." He sighed deeply. "I try, but I can't make her happy alone, Palu. I've tried, God knows." He turned back to the bookcase, overcome with frustration and unfocused rage. "I can't take care of her or give her what she needs."

"Nat." Palu spoke quietly but firmly from directly behind him. Nat felt his hand on his shoulder, a solid, gentle caress. He turned to see Palu looking at him with compassion and concern. It twisted his gut and made him more confused and angry than before. He tried to shake off his hand, but Palu's grip tightened and he held fast.

"Nat, Alecia loves you, more than you know, I think."

Nat snorted in disgust. "Yes, and a lot of good it's done her."

Palu grabbed Nat's shoulders with both hands and he shook him. "Don't disparage that, Nat. Don't cheapen how she feels for you. She's a grown woman and she's given you her love. That is a treasure beyond price."

It was Nat's turn to grab Palu's arms. He shoved his hands away, but he didn't let go of Palu's arms. He held on tightly trying to make him understand and desperately hoping that he wouldn't. "Do you think I don't know that? It isn't Alecia or her love that I question. It is me, Palu. I am the inadequate one here."

Palu tugged free and pulled Nat into a tight embrace. Nat wrapped his arms around Palu's chest and dug his fingers into his back. He buried his face in the freshly shaved skin of his neck and inhaled. Palu smelled like him. He'd used Nat's shaving soap, and his scent on Palu made Nat feel possessive and hungry and despondent. What was he doing?

Palu pressed his lips to the side of Nat's hair, his breath ruffling the hair over his ear, making Nat shiver. "Nat you are everything someone could wish for. You are intelligent and kind, amusing, handsome, generous. Should I go on? If I were Alecia I would feel as she does. I would do anything for you, Nat. Anything."

Nat felt lightheaded. Did Palu feel that way, too? Or was he just talking about Alecia? He rested his forehead on Palu's shoulder. Did it matter? Palu was leaving, they'd known that from that start. And Nat had always said he wouldn't do this. He wouldn't let himself care for a man. Palu was a lover, nothing more. A temporary distraction. They might like each other, they may have a great many things in common, but that didn't change the fact that they were both men, and that Nat and Alecia were married. Nat wouldn't hurt anyone like he'd seen Derek Knightly and even Tony Richards hurt. They'd been shut out in public, relegated to bachelor "friend" for the benefit of social acceptance. Did they feel as if their love was unimportant? Palu deserved more. He deserved someone who would claim him boldly and proudly, and Nat and Alecia couldn't do that.

He pushed Palu away roughly, surprising him. Palu stumbled back a step against the bookcase. Nat fell on him, pinning him there with his hips, his hands flattened against the books on either side of Palu's shoulders. "You don't understand," he growled, frustrated beyond belief at his inability to convey his real meaning to Palu.

Palu settled back against the bookcase calmly, not at all disturbed by Nat's aggression. "You keep saying that. Explain it to me."

Nat shook his head, the words stuck in his throat. How could he explain that they were using him? That because there could never be more between them, they were going to use Palu for their own ends? How could he adequately describe how sick and angry it made him that he had no other choice?

It didn't matter. What any of them felt in this situation made no difference at all. Things were what they were. All that mattered was the desire between them, the physical satisfaction they could give one another for a brief time. That's all there was and all there ever could be.

"This needs no explanation," he whispered, staring at Palu's mouth. He had a vision of Palu as he'd been just that morning, his mouth buried between Alecia's legs, pulling back with lips gleaming, and Nat had licked those lips clean, eaten all the sweet cream of Alecia's passion from Palu's full, sensuous mouth. He leaned in to kiss Palu and the other man twisted as if to avoid the contact.

"No, Nat, we need to talk—"

Nat ignored him. He grabbed a fistful of rough, curly hair and Palu's protest turned to a groan. Nat smiled darkly. He'd learned quite a bit about how to please Palu in the last day and a half. "Don't tell me no," Nat growled.

Palu's eyes were gleaming with heat and he narrowed them as he stared at Nat. "No," he said quite clearly.

Nat's smile grew. Apparently Palu had learned a thing or two about pleasing him, too. Palu suddenly spun Nat around and slammed him against the bookcase, rattling the books and knocking over a little figurine of a shepherdess. As it shattered on the floor the two men smiled grimly at each other as if in challenge. And then Palu swooped in and tried to take control of their kiss. Nat nearly let him. Christ, the man could kiss.

Palu drove his tongue into Nat's mouth and ate at him like a starving man. He wrapped his arms around Nat's middle and dragged him close, holding him so tightly Nat could barely breathe. Nat drove both hands into Palu's hair and tugged, hard. Palu grunted but he didn't move an inch. Instead he bit Nat's lower lip roughly until Nat whimpered and lessened the tension on Palu's hair. Palu rewarded him by gentling the kiss, licking Nat's lips and tangling sensuously with Nat's tongue. Nat groaned at the pleasure. Palu tasted sweet, like mint toothpowder, but the flavor was mixed with something wild that was distinctly Palu. Nat was beginning to crave that flavor, and that would never do.

With that thought Nat rolled until Palu's back hit the bookcase and he deepened the kiss again. He made it about lust, about sexual gratification and not about emotions. It couldn't be about emotions.

Palu surrendered, letting Nat control the kiss and control him. Nat shoved a knee between Palu's legs and the other man groaned when his thigh made contact with his groin. Palu's hands gripped Nat's hips, pulling him in and grinding against him. Yes, this is what they had. Nat had never had better with a man. Palu fit all his curves, provided pressure in all the right places.

Nat broke away with a gasp, staring at Palu with defiant satisfaction. Palu's eyes were glazed, his lips swollen and wet, his cheeks flushed. Nat was in control here. He was back in control. He nudged Palu's cock with his thigh, and looked down to see the outline of his rigid length straining against his tight breeches. The knowledge of what Palu hid under his clothes, his sensual and mesmerizing *tatau*, a thick cock covered in black ink, his bulging biceps decorated with primitive swirls and bands, drove Nat mad with lust. That was all his right now.

Nat watched as he ground his cock into Palu's through their clothes. He slowly swiveled his hips, rubbing against Palu, and Palu swore under his breath at the same time he gripped Nat's hips tighter, and held him closer.

"Is this what you want?" Nat whispered, looking away from their grinding hips. He stared into Palu's eyes, daring him to deny it. "Is this what you want to talk about?"

"No," Palu said through clenched teeth. "I don't want to talk about fucking. I just want you to fuck me."

The shiver that coursed down Nat's spine had nothing to do with the tumult of emotions inside him and everything to do with possession and desire and an overwhelming need to see this big man laid out below him, taking him in that gorgeous, marked bottom of his.

But not now. Not here. They had things to do.

"If you're a very good boy," Nat told Palu with a wicked smile, "I just might do that later."

Palu growled wordlessly, thrusting against Nat and Nat laughed. "Eager are we?"

"I don't know," Palu responded as he made Nat suck in a breath as he rubbed against him, "are we?"

Palu tried to kiss him again but Nat jerked away. He could see the surprise in Palu's face. He knew how much Nat enjoyed kissing him. But right now it felt too intimate. Nat had gotten their encounter where he wanted it, away from confessions and back to fucking. Kissing would destroy what little progress he'd made.

Just then Alecia walked into the drawing room. She took in the situation in one glance and quickly turned to close the door behind her before the servants saw what was going on. When she turned back to them she was smiling apprehensively.

"I'm sorry. I didn't mean to interrupt."

Nat put his hands on the bookcase and shoved away from Palu, who let him go immediately. "You didn't," Nat said nonchalantly. "We were just passing the time." He didn't look at Palu. He felt rather than saw Palu's withdrawal, his retreat into that polite expression that hid his thoughts. It was better this way, for all of them.

"Are you ready to go, my dear?" he asked Alecia.

She paled slightly and bit her lip before answering. "Are you sure you still wish to go, Natty?"

"Of course," he said with a frown at her. She mustn't lose her courage now. This time it would work. He was sure of it. He pushed his own disquiet down deep and focused on what had to be done. "We always go to tea with your parents on the second Tuesday of the month."

"What?" Palu exclaimed, his confusion evident.

"Surely you don't mind accompanying us?" Nat asked as he stopped in front of a small mirror to adjust his cravat and lapels. He was finding it unbearable not to look at Palu. Christ, what a bloody fucking awful day this was going to be.

"Alecia?" Palu asked from behind. Nat spun around to pin her with a hard stare. She kept her gaze on Nat, blinking rapidly.

"Yes?" Her voice was thin. Would Palu notice?

"Do you wish me to go?"

She turned to Palu, her expression troubled. "I don't want you to leave us." Her answer was ambiguous, Nat had to give her credit for that. He knew she wasn't in favor of his plan, but she would do as he asked because she trusted him. Please God, Nat prayed, let it work this time. For once let him make the right decision for them. He'd almost turned away when he caught the longing in her gaze as she stared at Palu. Perhaps her answer hadn't been so ambiguous then. She truly did not want Palu to leave them. But the journey had to end somewhere. Nat was afraid he knew their destination today might very well be their final one.

* * * * *

"More tea, Mr. Anderson?"

Alecia's mother, Mrs. Colby, was as petite as her daughter. She was shy as well, but in a different way from Alecia. She was a timid mouse, overwhelmed by her domineering husband. Perhaps she might have outgrown it if she hadn't been tied to a man who wanted to keep her that way.

Palu wasn't exactly sure why he was here. He and Nat and Alecia had spent almost two days making love and laughing, and the next thing he knew they'd bundled him up and brought him here to tea with the father who hated them. His head was spinning, especially after that confusing conversation with Nat this morning. There was no sign of the laughing Englishman who had entranced him at Wilchester's the other night.

"No, thank you, ma'am," Palu replied politely. He tried not to sigh at her flinch as he spoke. He could tell he made her nervous. He'd seen it a hundred times before, in as many drawing rooms. It didn't matter that he'd been raised in England, had the finest education, and was a prominent scholar. All they saw was his brown skin and broad nose and coarse hair and they feared his primitive nature. To be sure, outside of the bedroom Palu didn't think he had much of a primitive nature. He was a rather easygoing fellow if people bothered to get to know him. He'd actually been surprised to discover his primitive sexual nature with Nat and Alecia. He smiled into his cup as he took a sip of tea. They didn't seem to fear the savage.

Nat was prowling the perimeter of the room. It was clear he did not enjoy being here, which made their visit all the more puzzling, since he'd insisted on it. Alecia sat to Palu's left, biting her lip and fiddling with her teacup. Her father sat in solitary splendor in an ornate chair beneath a large portrait of himself above the empty fireplace. It was quite Gothic, and

Palu would have laughed except that he feared no one else would understand the joke.

"What do you want?" Mr. Colby bit out. Palu was startled and turned to him, but he was speaking to Nat.

Nat turned to Colby with a sneer. "You know what we want. What we always want. It is you who make us appear here every month to grovel for what is rightfully ours. If you do not wish to see us, then give us the whole sum."

Palu was shocked beyond speech. Even though Alecia had told him, he hadn't actually expected Nat and Mr. Colby to be so hostile to one another. It appeared as if Nat wished to shoot Mr. Colby as much as the older man wanted to shoot Nat. And what sum was he talking about?

"Is she with child?" Mr. Colby sneered back. "Or have you not managed that yet?" He pointed a shaking finger at Palu. "Is this your attempt at blackmail? Are you going to have him get a babe on her? To shame us?"

"What?" Palu exclaimed. Good Lord, one simply did not discuss these things in the drawing room over tea. He glanced at Alecia and saw her cheeks were stained with mortification. She wouldn't look at him.

"You know the doctors said she will not conceive again," Nat ground out. "Do you not think it pains us both? Must you grind our noses in it?"

Again? Palu was shocked and dismayed. Nat and Alecia had lost a baby? When?

Mr. Colby's lips thinned with anger until they disappeared. "She lost the babe because of her whoring for you."

Mrs. Colby gasped and Palu saw her lips tremble. He had to grit his teeth against the angry words stuck in his throat.

"Enough," Alecia said in a shaking voice. "We have come for our monthly allowance, Father," she said, clenching her hands in her lap. "Nat is right. If you would just give us the funds in my dowry, we would not all have to endure this monthly torture."

"You call visiting your mother torture?" Mr. Colby asked in anger.

"No, Father. I would gladly visit with Mother." She didn't need to add that she did not wish to see her father. The unspoken sentiment was understood by all.

Mr. Colby's face turned a darker shade of red. "I am not required to turn the money over until you are thirty years old," he said coldly. "I feel it is my duty to keep control of it until then. You and your husband have no sense of responsibility or decorum. To give you the money now to waste on your hedonistic pleasures would be folly, and a disservice to you."

Nat scoffed. "You wish to control us with your parsimonious guardianship. Surely you know that is not going to happen."

Again Mr. Colby pointed a shaking finger at Palu. "You didn't answer my question. Why is he here?"

Palu was wondering the same thing. There was a cold suspicion creeping through his veins. All his ludicrous and emotional speculations the last two days seemed to ridicule him from every angle. He tried to catch their eyes, but neither Nat nor Alecia would look at him. He put his cup down, afraid it would rattle in his shaking hands.

"Mr. Anderson is a recent acquaintance," Nat said calmly. "We have been spending a great deal of time together. I'm sure that it will soon be common knowledge."

Mr. Colby stood and Palu saw Alecia biting her lip so hard he was afraid she would make herself bleed. But why was he worried about her? Was he such a fool?

"Unless I pay you, is that right?" Mr. Colby accused. "You resort to blackmail now? If I don't wish it to be common knowledge that my daughter is consorting with this savage, I must bow to your demands."

Palu stood and all eyes turned to him. Alecia's eyes were red and swimming with unshed tears. He could see the plea in their pretty brown depths. When he looked at Nat all he saw was anger. But when Nat glanced at Alecia Palu saw the regret and determination in his eyes. Palu turned to Mr. Colby.

"Yes," he said. With that one word he threw his own pride aside. He knew he'd been used by them. But they had certainly given of themselves as well. He saw no shame in returning the favor. This was a situation beyond their control. Alecia had alluded several times to their lack of funds, for traveling and other pursuits. Palu hadn't understood, obviously. He hadn't understood what Nat was telling him this morning, either. Now he did.

Mr. Colby glared at him. "Blackmail is a punishable offense," he spit out.

Palu merely smiled politely. "One that requires the victim to admit what he is being blackmailed about," he answered. "And I do not think that is what you wish."

Mr. Colby regarded him for a moment and then sat with a cold smile. "Fine. Tell them." He waved vaguely in the direction of the street. "Tell them all. It is not I who will be hurt by the gossip. I will deposit the usual monthly allowance in their account. But no more." He looked down and brushed at something on his lapel. "But if it does become known that my daughter has...befriended you, then I will have to forbid them from coming to this house again." Mrs. Colby gave a little hiccup of distress, and Mr. Colby silenced her with a glare. "I will not have my house tainted by association."

Palu started to speak, but Alecia cut him off. "No. No more." She stood and in her distress nearly lost her balance. Palu stepped quickly to her side and she placed her hand on his arm. The contact produced a shiver of awareness. He smiled grimly. His body clearly hadn't caught up with the current situation.

"Goodbye, Mother," Alecia said. Mrs. Colby glanced at her husband, but then she stood and grabbed Alecia's hand. Palu could see how tightly she held it. She kissed Alecia's cheek.

"Goodbye, my dear," she whispered. She sat quickly, not looking at Palu or Nat.

Nat stalked over to the door and opened it. He glared at Mr. Colby. "This is not over," he promised.

Mr. Colby sneered at him. "Yes, I do believe it is. I have called your bluff. You will do nothing to harm Alecia, Digby. You have made the fatal error of falling in love with her. I pity you."

They were shown out of the house, Nat simmering with barely controlled rage. Palu was numb. Could he have been so wrong about them? When they reached the street Alecia stood there with her eyes downcast and her hands clasped tightly in front of her. Palu stopped next to her, his hand on her elbow polite, but nothing more. They waited for the carriage to be brought around. Nat paced a few feet away at the street's edge.

"Palu—" Alecia began in a voice filled with tears.

"Not here," he interrupted. He pulled his handkerchief out and handed it to her. Neither of them looked at the other. When the carriage arrived Palu hesitated to enter.

"Get in," Nat barked. He threw himself against the seat back and stared out the window next to him, his face turned away from Palu. Palu climbed in, more as a courtesy than anything else. He supposed they all deserved a better end than this.

Alecia seemed the better choice of traveling companion, and Palu sat down next to her. The carriage lurched into traffic and Palu waited.

Alecia broke first. "I'm so sorry," she cried, sniffling into his handkerchief. "It wasn't supposed to be like that. It wasn't supposed to be so...so ugly."

Nat leaned his forearms on his thighs, turning his hat in his hands between his knees. He sighed deeply. "No, no it wasn't."

"Exactly what did you expect it to be?" Palu asked dispassionately. He was feeling very little at that moment. He had a terrible premonition the feelings would come later, when he was alone.

Nat fell back against the seat again. "I don't know," he cried. "It was a stupid, foolish thing to do." He finally looked at Palu, and there was genuine regret and confusion in his face. "I just thought..." He sighed again. "Hell, I don't know what I thought."

"Why do you need the money?" If it was for something important, something that meant life or death, then he could understand it. He could forgive them.

"Nat, he wants to travel," Alecia said, blowing her nose. "He's more than an amateur naturalist. He's brilliant, Palu, really," she said earnestly, begging him with her eyes to believe her. "He deserves the chance. The money, it's ours. It belongs to me, my dowry. But they put something in the contracts, Nat's father and mine, so that we can't get to it until I'm thirty." She slumped in the seat, as if she'd lost the will to convince him. "He's stuck here with me," she murmured, looking away.

"It's not for me, Lee," Nat argued passionately. "I would do anything to get you away from here, away from him. To give you the world. Anything." He reached out and clutched her hand still holding the handkerchief. "We'll find another way."

Alecia shook her head. "No, Nat, we won't. He's got us and he knows it. By the time I'm thirty most of the money will be gone. He's not investing it at all." She wiped her nose. "He's got it all planned. He'll still hold the purse strings, and we'll never be free then."

Palu felt a strange pity for them. They'd used him abominably, but he couldn't hate them for it. They'd done it for each other. He'd always known that it was all about Nat and Alecia, hadn't he? Nat's confession this morning about his inadequacy and his inability to take care of Alecia made perfect sense now.

"And your family?" he asked Nat.

Nat shook his head. "I'm the third son of a viscount, and not a well-to-do one." He snorted inelegantly. "My allowance barely pays for the coachman."

"I'm sorry I couldn't be of more help," Palu said, and he meant it to a degree.

Nat looked at him incredulously. "Sorry? Palu we were horrid to even use you this way. You were more of a gentleman than you had to be, standing up with us. You've nothing to be sorry for. We are the ones who are sorry." His look changed to speculation. "Why did you do it?"

Palu shrugged and hid his hurt under a polite smile. "You certainly gave me all that I asked for and more in the last two days. I could not refuse to return the favor."

Alecia bit her lip and Nat blushed. "The last two days, those had nothing to do with this," Nat told him roughly.

Palu laughed, and this time he couldn't disguise all the bitterness. "They had everything to do with it. Did you plan it from the start, before you approached us at the ball?"

"No!" Alecia cried out, grabbing his arm. "No, we just wanted you, that was all."

"I see," Palu replied. "And when did your desire change?"

"Our desire never changed," Nat told him sharply. "But I didn't see the harm in scaring Colby a little. He's already embarrassed by us among his pious friends."

Well, that hurt, having Nat confirm that Palu was the equivalent of the bogeyman. "When did you decide this?" That's what he couldn't figure out. They'd been together every minute since they'd met.

"Yesterday," Alecia said softly, "when you were...indisposed."

"Ah," Palu said, amused in spite of everything. "Well, that will teach me to seek privacy at my own risk."

88

The carriage slowed and Palu looked out to see that they'd arrived back at Nat and Alecia's. After they disembarked, Palu bowed politely. "Thank you for an enjoyable two days."

"Palu, please," Alecia begged earnestly, "don't leave like this, please. Come in with us. Let us talk."

He couldn't. Not now. He was too confused and too hurt. He was afraid what he might reveal. He shook his head.

"Tonight," Nat said, his voice brooking no argument. "You'll come back tonight."

Palu smiled politely again and tipped his hat. "I have business that I have left unattended for the last two days that I must see to. I cannot make it before, let us say nine o'clock. Will that satisfy you?"

Nat nodded grimly and Alecia worried her lip with her teeth. Palu reached out and gently pulled on her lower lip with his thumb until she let it go. "Until tonight then," he said quietly. He turned and walked away, cursing himself for the fool he was.

Nat waited until he and Alecia were alone in their bedroom before he spoke. "I was wrong. I never should have suggested it. We've hurt him, I think." His heart was heavy in his chest.

He hadn't felt this badly since Alecia had cried and told him how much he'd hurt her with his constant string of lovers. It was when she lost the babe. They'd only known about it for a short while before she lost it. But when it happened, it had ripped a hole in both of them and they'd lashed out. When the grief passed, they had spoken of things that had long festered under the surface, and they'd been closer than ever before. But Nat never forgot the feeling of desolation he'd had knowing that he'd hurt her so badly.

He stopped short, unable to breathe for the realization choking him. He cared. In spite of all his precautions, in spite of the warnings he'd given himself over and over, he cared for Palu, cared that he was hurt.

"Oh Nat," Alecia cried. She sat down on the edge of the bed and covered her face with her hands. "I hate myself right now." She shook her head and sobbed. "I never wanted to hurt him. He's so sweet, and funny, and...and tender, and he *feels*, Natty, he cares. No one has ever really cared."

Nat was torn. Should he confess to Alecia that he had feelings for Palu? Or would that open all the old wounds again? They were happy now, well, not now, but in their marriage, happy with each other. He couldn't imagine not loving Alecia. She was his best friend, his most ardent supporter. She thought him brilliant and witty and exciting. If he were to lose her love and admiration, how could he go on?

But he had to tell her. Secrets had no place between them. "Alecia," he choked out. He stumbled over to the bed and sat next to her, pulling her into his arms. He hugged her tightly and whispered fiercely against her hair. "I think I'm falling in love with him."

Alecia froze for a moment and then she gasped and hugged him back. "Oh, Natty, so am I. So am I."

"What are we going to do now?" he asked her softly. She had no answers, and neither did he. Once again Nat had made the wrong choices for them and hurt Alecia in the process. Would he never get it right?

Chapter Seven

ဢ

Alecia didn't like the way Hardington was looking at her. She glanced at the clock. He'd only been here five minutes and she wished him gone. To hell, preferably. When Soames had announced they had a visitor she'd thought for one breathless moment that perhaps Palu had reconsidered. She was dismayed to find out it was Hardington. Ever since she and Nat had entertained Hardington about a year ago, he'd been hounding them to take him to their bed again. He had become a nuisance, and Nat had stopped being polite in his refusals.

They hadn't enjoyed their night with Hardington, and they'd cut it short, seeing him out the door after less than two hours. He was vain and selfish, both in bed and out. Unfortunately they hadn't known that prior to their invitation. He was handsome and charming when he wanted to be. He had not chosen to be so when he was in bed with them. He made demands, pouted when he didn't get what he wanted, and cared nothing for Nat or Alecia's pleasure.

"So you've shown Anderson the door, have you?" Hardington asked with satisfaction as he sat down on the sofa across from her and Nat. "I rather thought his appeal would wear off quickly. One needs more than brute strength and curiosity value to satisfy lovers such as you."

"What are you talking about?" Nat snapped. He'd hesitated when Soames had announced Hardington. He'd wanted the butler to tell him that Nat and Alecia were not at home, which had suited Alecia. But he'd decided they should see him and make perfectly clear that they were not interested in any further liaisons with him.

91

Hardington scoffed. "Please. It was painfully obvious when you left Wilchester's the other night that the three of you could not wait to fuck one another."

Nat stood abruptly. "I think you should leave, Hardington. And we do not wish you to come back, ever. I thought we had made *that* painfully obvious. But clearly you are too thick to understand my too-polite refusals. We do not want you. We do not want to see you. Do not come back. If you do, we will be unavailable even for conversation."

Hardington's face was tight with anger and something else. Jealousy? Speculation? Alecia wasn't sure, but she knew she didn't like the looks of it. Hardington adjusted his seat on the sofa and crossed one leg over the other, resting his ankle on his knee. He ignored Nat's dismissal.

"So you've developed a taste for the native, have you? He must be as good as they say." The last was said with sneering sarcasm, and Alecia found her temper rising.

"He is a better man than you could ever hope to be," she said heatedly, "in bed and out."

Hardington's jaw flexed as if he were grinding his teeth. "He has a difficult time here in England, you know." His tone was deceptively mild. "I'd hate to see it get harder for him, seeing as how he's such a sterling fellow."

Nat crossed his arms. "Now what are you blathering about?"

"I have it on good authority that there were quite a few members of the Royal Society, patrons and scholars alike, who did not support Anderson's election as a Fellow. It was only Sir Joseph Banks' intercession that assured his election."

Alecia felt a chill and rubbed her arms. "Why are you telling us this?"

"There are several patrons of the Society who would not be happy to learn of Anderson's rather unusual entertainments." Hardington looked intently at both of them. "It would be wise for him to cease those activities if he wishes the Society to remain ignorant of them."

Alecia almost laughed at the irony of the situation. This morning they had attempted blackmail and were unsuccessful because of their feelings for one another. This afternoon they would give in to blackmail because of their feelings for Palu. Certainly the God of justice had a wicked sense of humor.

"You wouldn't dare try to tarnish his reputation," Nat snarled. "The destruction of your own would not be far behind."

Hardington's laugh was genuinely amused. "I am not Anderson. He wears sin like a crown of thorns."

"Meaning what?" Nat growled.

Hardington looked amused. "Come now, his dark, savage looks incline people to think the worst of him. You know it is true." He held a hand to his chest and looked innocently at them. "Whereas I am the epitome of a well-respected English gentleman."

"Why are you doing this?" Alecia whispered.

Hardington looked surprised for a moment. Then he smiled grimly. "I'm tired of losing to Anderson. He had a lover during the war, you know, a very pretty boy named William. William had a choice between me and that savage. He chose Anderson." He took several deep breaths in rising anger. "And now you two."

"Perhaps if you weren't such a bastard, Hardington, someone would choose you," Nat said, hatred dripping from every word.

Hardington's smile was malicious. "But more importantly he has cost me money. A great deal of money." He leaned back and spread his arms across the back of the sofa.

"What money? How?" Nat demanded.

"I wished to invest in his little excursions to the South Seas," Hardington bit out. "Exploration in that area has turned out to be rather lucrative. He turned me down." He frowned fiercely. "I would have made enough money to buy you both, and several more like you."

Alecia felt the color drain from her face. Is this how others saw them? As whores to be bought?

"No amount of money would have made us choose you, Hardington," Nat growled.

"You are going to choose me," Hardington informed them smugly. "If you want to save your precious Anderson, you will."

Alecia bit her lip, horrified. God, she just couldn't. She couldn't have relations with Hardington now. Not ever. But for Palu...she cut her gaze to Nat who was glaring at the other man. He didn't say anything, however.

Hardington laughed and got up from the sofa. He took two steps across to the settee on which Alecia sat and lowered himself down next to her, close enough that their sides were pressed together as he put his arm around her. He leaned in and kissed her on the neck, and she looked away, tears burning in her eyes. She supposed Nat would have to do it, too, to keep Hardington quiet. She closed her eyes and thought of Palu as Hardington's hand began to inch up her thigh and he bit her neck none too gently.

Suddenly her arm was grabbed and she was ripped out of Hardington's grasp and into Nat's arms. She clung to him, relief swamping her. "Neither my wife nor I will whore for you, Hardington," he said coldly. "My previous answer still stands. We do not wish to see you again. Ever. Get the hell out of my house."

Hardington sighed. "I thought you might say that." He stood and straightened the lapels of his coat. "But it was worth a try." His smile was still superior. "However, I do not think you will turn down my alternative offer."

"Get out," Nat ground out.

Hardington snorted under his breath. "I don't know why I bother." He snapped his fingers. "Oh, yes I do. Revenge." He walked over to the drawing room doors and turned to regard them. "He'll leave soon, you realize. England does not agree with him. If you stay away from him until his departure I shall not report your association to the Society."

Alecia at first felt relief, but then the full impact of his words hit her. "Never see Palu again?" she asked incredulously.

"Palu?" Hardington appeared confused and then he barked with laughter. "Is he calling himself by some absurd native name now? How utterly ridiculous he is." He nodded at Alecia. "That is correct, my dear. Never see — what did you call him, Palu? — again."

Nat's arms tightened around her. "Do you swear it, Hardington? If we stay away from Mr. Anderson you will not carry tales to the Society?"

Hardington bowed mockingly. "I swear it." He rose and his smile was polite, his manner impeccable. "And I will have neatly accomplished both his punishment and yours for refusing me. It is a neat little package, don't you think?"

Nat sighed in disgust. "He is indeed a very intelligent man."

Hardington lost his polished manners. "Mock if you will, Digby. But I shall be the one laughing in the end." He opened the doors and began to leave, but stopped in the doorway and turned back to them. "Do not try to see him again, not even once, or I shall make sure tales of his adventures with you reach the appropriate ears."

He closed the doors on Nat's curse and Alecia's tears. Nat lowered Alecia to the settee, but she didn't want to sit there anymore, where Hardington had touched her. She scampered over to a high backed chair before the window. She sniffed loudly, trying to stop her tears. Tears weren't going to accomplish anything, and she'd already cried a bucket today. Nat was sitting at the small escritoire in the corner, writing something.

"What are you doing?" Alecia asked in a watery voice. She sniffed again. Nat reached behind him holding out his handkerchief to her. She got up and took it and then she peered over his shoulder.

"'Dear Mr. Anderson,'" she read, her voice wavering, "'It is with regret that we must cancel our engagement this evening. Events have unfolded that make it impossible to ascertain when we might see you again. Please accept our apologies. Nat and Alecia Digby.'"

"Oh, Natty!" she cried, trying to grab the paper. "It's so cold. Can't you just tell him what has happened?"

Nat held it out of her reach. "Are you mad? He'll come storming over and attempt to protect us from Hardington, not caring a fig for his own reputation." Nat turned and gripped her hand tightly. "Don't you see, Lee? The Society is all he has here in England. It is all that makes them accept him here. If he were to lose that…we can't let that happen, Lee. We have to protect him. You know we do." Nat's grip loosened and he slumped in the chair. "Besides, what else can we expect from him? We used him terribly this morning. We hurt his feelings and betrayed his trust. There is no way he can forgive us. The shadow of our betrayal and the specter of discovery would always follow us. There is no future for him with us." Nat looked at her beseechingly. "We'll be all right, Lee. We still have each other, don't we? We shall be all right."

Yes, Alecia silently agreed as Nat laid his cheek against her stomach and she hugged him to her. They would be all right, but they would never be the same.

* * * * *

"What do you want, Hardington?" Palu asked in a tired voice. Hardington was the last person he wished to deal with today.

"Is that any way to greet an old friend?" Hardington replied pleasantly, flipping out his coattails as he took a seat in the chair across from Palu's desk.

"No, but then you hardly classify as such," Palu said dryly. "You barely warrant a listing under acquaintance."

Hardington held a hand to his chest in mock distress. "You wound me, Anderson."

Palu sighed in resignation. Clearly Hardington was in a strange mood. "State your business, Hardington," he asked again. "Why are you here?"

"Why, I've just come to visit," Hardington declared. "It seems that once again our interests have traveled in the same direction, and I thought we should compare research notes."

Hardington laughed as if at a jest, but Palu was merely confused. "You wish to see my research notes?"

Hardington continued to laugh as he shook his head. "Good God, you didn't actually take notes while you were fucking them, did you?"

Palu's breath caught in his chest. "What?" he choked out.

"Nat and Alecia, of course," Hardington said, as if speaking to a simpleton. "I heard that you got a taste of what all London raves about." He grinned mischievously. "I know I certainly gave them high marks after our affair."

Oh God. Palu tried to school his features into a mask of calm disinterest, but he knew he was failing miserably by the glee on Hardington's face.

"Oh, dear, don't tell me you thought that your encounter with them was something special?" Hardington said in tones of exaggerated sympathy. "Although perhaps it was, considering who and what you are. I'm sure they've never fucked anyone like you." He paused for a moment. "Palu."

Palu's hands were clenched tightly around the end of his chair arms. "I was unaware that their entertainments were quite so lavishly attended as to include all of London," Palu replied, rather proud of how even his voice was. "But, no, I did not think that I was the first to enjoy them." Inside he was reeling. They'd spoken with Hardington about their nights together. They'd even told him Palu's real name, something only a handful of people knew.

"Well, you were the talk of London, Palu," Hardington told him with delight, "so it's no wonder they pounced before someone else got you first."

"Anderson," Palu replied automatically. The sound of his name from Hardington's mouth made his gut roil in revulsion.

"Oh?" Hardington said with a pout. "I suppose only those who get to fuck you are allowed to call you by your primitive name."

"What do you want?" Palu asked again. He knew Hardington, knew his type. He did nothing without a selfish motive.

"Want? Why nothing!" he exclaimed jovially. "I really did just want to gossip about the experience. I mean, they are very good, aren't they? And Alecia certainly loves to watch her husband fuck another man, doesn't she?"

Palu thought he might throw up. He didn't dare risk answering for fear of embarrassing himself.

"And Alecia, she's so tiny, I was always afraid of hurting her." Hardington smirked. "But she likes that, so it isn't really a problem."

Palu took several deep breaths through his nose to fight the nausea.

"Did you get Nat to suck your cock?" Hardington said in a stage whisper, leaning toward the desk conspiratorially. "You really ought to, if you can. He simply loves to do it."

98

Palu stood abruptly. "I do not understand why you are telling me these things," he ground out.

Hardington stood as well with a sigh. "Anderson, believe it or not I have come with a word of advice." He held up a hand as Palu started to give a sarcastic retort. "No, listen to me, I beseech you." He walked around to sit on the edge of Palu's desk next to where he stood. "Nat is a bit of an amateur naturalist, you know," he said, watching Palu carefully. When he showed no reaction, Hardington continued. "He has long been fascinated with your writings and your travels. I'm sure the chance to fuck the strange and mysterious half-breed Anderson was irresistible to him. And Alecia, of course. She follows where Nat leads, but she has some…unusual appetites of her own." Hardington rose with a weary sigh and turned toward the door. "I know you do not like me, Anderson," he told him compassionately, "but I have always had a bit of a tendre for you, which you well know." He smiled deprecatingly. "I may not be able to have you, but I do not want to see you hurt." He held up a hand beseechingly. "You are naught but a curiosity to them, and I would hate to have tales of your sexual exploits with them bandied about London, as if you were some freak of nature to be studied and discussed."

Palu could barely breathe for the disillusionment coursing through his veins. All his old fears were justified, his oddity made obvious. How had he not seen it? They had been so fascinated with his *tatau*, his primitive nature, his travels. He was nothing but an experiment to them, a curiosity. He'd already felt used by them, but now the feeling was tenfold. Would he never learn? Would he always find betrayal wherever he gave trust?

"I'm sorry, Anderson," Hardington said, his words belied by the satisfied gleam in his eyes. That he should be the one to tell Palu these things doubled the perfidy of Nat and Alecia's behavior.

Palu remained silent, and Hardington tipped his hat and left the room, closing the door quietly behind him. As soon as it shut Palu sat gracelessly in his chair, shaken by the enormity of his disappointment. He had thought at last he'd found someone he could call his own. Yesterday he had actually entertained thoughts of falling in love with them. Then the morning encounter with Colby, and now this. He had become a fool while he'd been sailing the world.

He shook his head as he looked out the window at the grim, overcast day. It suited his mood perfectly, but not his person. He shivered. He was not made for England, or the deceits of Englishmen. The sooner he put his affairs in order the better. He would notify the captain of his ship to find a crew and prepare to sail in two months time. He could tolerate two months if it meant never having to see these shores again.

When Palu received Nat and Alecia's note an hour later he was relieved. He had not wanted to see them again, but he had not known what to write when he sat down to pen a note canceling their meeting. Now he would not need to. In a strange way, the note ending their affair so quickly and neatly made him think better of Nat and Alecia. They did not plan to deceive him and continue their affair based on lies. Clearly they had gotten what they wanted from him. If only Palu could say the same.

Chapter Eight

∞

"I cannot remember that last time I walked Hyde Park as if it were a graveyard," Simon lamented. "May we at least know the reason for your moribund countenance?"

Palu's laugh was forced. "That bad, am I?"

It had been a week since he'd received Nat and Alecia's note, but still he could not forget their time together. He tortured himself nightly with the memories. His work and lectures at the Royal Society did not occupy him as he'd thought they would. Everything reminded him of Nat and Alecia and what could have been. He hadn't been able to resist asking people at the Society about them. He'd discovered that Nat was indeed a respected amateur naturalist, avidly reading everything the members published and loyally attending lectures. He was well-liked among Palu's peers, none of whom spoke a negative word about Nat and Alecia's personal life.

Palu had avoided social engagements, but drinking himself into a stupor each night wasn't helping either. When Daniel had sent a note around asking him to walk in the park today, he'd readily accepted. Perhaps his old friend could take his mind off them.

"Come," Daniel said, turning off the main path to sit on an unoccupied bench. He patted the seat next to him. "Tell me what is wrong, Palu."

"Palu?" Simon asked, walking around to stand behind the bench as Palu sat.

"It is an old childhood name," Palu replied, desultorily watching the carriages and people pass by, showing off their latest gowns and conquests at the fashionable hour. "It is the name my mother gave me."

"I thought your name was Gregory?" Simon sounded only vaguely interested. A glance confirmed that he was busy smiling and flirting with a carriage full of blushing young women and an old harridan who kept slapping the poor girls' wrists with her fan, admonishing them as they waved at acquaintances.

"That is my English name."

Simon frowned and then smiled brightly. "Oh, are we all going to get native names? I should like that. How do you say huge in your native tongue, Anderson?" Simon leered lasciviously and thrust his hips suggestively at the carriage and Palu heard the women squeal in delight as the old woman bellowed with rage. Beside him Daniel sighed with weary resignation at Simon's antics.

"Palu," he answered dryly, and Simon looked at him blankly and then laughed.

"Oh, I say, that was a good one," Simon told him. "Palu. Huge. Very good."

"Thank you," Palu replied politely, amused in spite of his melancholy. The memory of Nat exclaiming how huge he was that first night wiped the amusement from his face.

"So Daniel calls you by your childhood name," Simon said, waving his fingers at the retreating carriage. "How long have you two known one another?"

"Since we were young children," Palu replied. "I cannot remember exactly when we met."

"Yes," Daniel agreed. "We were quite young, I believe, when our fathers became first correspondents and then acquaintances. My father was fascinated with Captain Cook's voyages and Mr. Anderson's discoveries." He smiled at Palu. "Do you remember Mr. Cadley?"

Palu laughed. "Our first tutor? Yes, I remember him, poor man. What a trial we were to him."

"So you were educated together?" Simon asked with interest. "At what school?"

102

Daniel shook his head. "No school. We had a private tutor, and of course Mr. Anderson taught us the natural sciences."

Simon looked agog at Daniel. "You were educated by one of the most brilliant scholars of our time and you've never mentioned it?"

Daniel shrugged. "I didn't say I learned all that he had to teach."

Palu shook his head and leaned forward to rest his arms on his knees, staring at the ground between his feet. "Nor did I," he agreed solemnly. "He tried to teach me to always be careful here. But I have never given that lesson the credence it deserves."

"Talk," Daniel ordered firmly. He settled deeper onto the bench, crossing his legs, ignoring the people parading through the park around them.

"I have simply had an affair that ended badly," Palu said dismissively. "I will get over it."

Simon leaned his arms on the back of the bench between Daniel and Palu and frowned at him. "Oh, I say, not Nat and Alecia, surely? I really thought that would work out."

"Let him finish, Simon," Daniel said patiently.

"I am finished," Palu told him. He had no wish to dissect his gullibility for Simon and Daniel's edification.

"Hardly," Daniel drawled. "What happened?"

Palu sighed. "I spent a couple of nights with them, that's all. They ended it."

"Why?" Daniel was still calm, but his voice was firm, and Palu knew from experience that Daniel would keep at him until he confessed all, damn his hide.

"I was merely a curiosity to them," he told them, looking away out over the throng of people to the green beyond. "And a means to an end."

"What are you talking about?" Simon asked sharply. "What did they tell you?"

Palu laughed bitterly. "Ah, it wasn't what they told me. It was where they took me." He glanced over at Daniel and the other man raised a brow in inquiry. "We had tea with Alecia's parents."

It took a moment but Palu could see the moment that Daniel put the facts together to reach a conclusion. He closed his eyes as if pained. "They didn't," he said, but it wasn't a question.

Palu nodded. "Yes, they did."

"What?" Simon asked in confusion. "Do you two have some sort of secret language? What happened?"

Palu leaned back against the bench in an inelegant sprawl. He didn't care about how he looked right now. "They attempted to blackmail her dowry out of her father by threatening to reveal our affair to everyone."

"Good God," Simon said in shock. "Those bloody stupid little..." He stopped with a sigh. His hand came down on Palu's shoulder and Palu looked at him. For once Simon appeared serious. "Don't judge them too harshly, Anderson. They are at a crossroads."

Palu frowned. "What do you mean?"

Daniel twirled his walking stick in the dirt in front of him, looking pensively across the park. "Since their reconciliation and the loss of their child, they have no direction. They live day to day, waiting on grudging handouts from her father, seeking the next man for their bed, hoping he's the one, and talking fervently of leaving it all behind."

Palu snorted. "So I am one of a string of many?"

Daniel looked at him sharply. "Is that how it felt?"

Palu couldn't deceive Daniel, he never could. He shook his head. "No." He took a deep breath and told him the rest. "But Hardington came to see me. Apparently Nat and Alecia have been talking about our time together, at least to him."

"Hardington?" Simon exclaimed. "Why on earth would they talk to Hardington?"

Palu shrugged. "Apparently he is also their lover. He told me that my value to them was as a curiosity, a figure of examination for two eager young scholars."

This time Simon cuffed him in the shoulder, nearly knocking Palu off the bench. "And you believed him, you idiot?"

Palu blinked at him. "What?"

Simon snorted in disgust. "Hardington has been trying to get into their bed for well over a year. Granted, he was there once, *one time*, and they have refused him since, much to his regret. He seethes every time they take a new lover and it isn't him."

That made Palu feel a little better. At least their standards were higher than Hardington.

Daniel didn't say a word, just continued to pensively tap his stick in the dirt.

"Hardington is up to something," Simon said with conviction. "I would place a bet on it."

"Well," Daniel said with a slight smile, "you'll not get any takers. That is a fool's bet. Hardington is always up to something."

Palu shook his head in disgust, this time at himself. "Yes, he is. And I know that, yet I let him convince me otherwise."

"Love makes fools of us all," Daniel said simply.

"Oh, I say, are you in love with them?" Simon asked incredulously. "Damn me, but I am good."

Palu had stopped paying attention. He had just spotted Nat and Alecia walking along the path. He stood and knew the instant they spotted him.

"We seem to have lost him again," Simon commented as he and Daniel watched Palu stand and stare down the lane at Nat and Alecia.

Daniel grinned. "So it would seem." He watched as Nat and Alecia slowly walked toward them as if in a trance. They didn't even spare a glance for Simon and Daniel, staring intently at Palu.

"Ugh," Simon commented dryly. "Not love again."

"Good afternoon," Alecia said quietly as she stopped in front of Palu, too close for propriety, but none of the three seemed to care. She stared up at him with hungry eyes, and Palu stood there, his head tilted down as his eyes devoured her.

"Good afternoon," Palu said just as quietly. He turned to look at Nat, who was watching Palu and Alecia like a starving man staring at a banquet.

"Good afternoon," Nat whispered.

"Good afternoon," Simon called out convivially, but the three ignored him. Daniel turned and frowned at him. Simon just shrugged with an amused grin.

"May I see you home?" Palu asked politely, although his dark, rough tone spoke of things that were not at all polite.

"Oh, yes, please," Alecia said breathlessly. They turned, Alecia clinging to Nat's arm, while Palu walked beside them, his hands clasped tightly behind his back.

Daniel watched them walk off with a small pang of jealousy. All around him people were falling in love. Too bad Daniel had done that long ago, and didn't seem capable of reproducing the feat.

"I'm rather alarmed at this new role of mother hen we seem to have adopted," Simon mused as he sat down next to Daniel and adjusted his coat as he smiled at a comely widow walking by. If Daniel remembered correctly Simon had slept with the widow for a month or two after the death of her husband.

"As am I," Daniel murmured. "I am hardly one to offer advice to the lovelorn."

Simon snorted. "Nonsense. You're a great one for giving advice. It's taking it that you fail at dismally."

"Says the man who can't seem to resist climbing into the bed of every grieving widow and wayward soul he can find, none of whom offer a future of any kind," Daniel returned sharply.

Simon looked at him with exaggerated confusion. "What on earth do my sexual escapades have to do with your inability to take advice on your unrequited, doomed love?"

Daniel stood abruptly. "You really can be a bastard, Simon." He dusted off his pants and began walking. Simon casually fell into step beside him.

"Of course I can," he agreed good-naturedly. "And I'm bloody good at it when I'm at my best. But don't ask my mother. She'll deny it."

"You are always at your best," Daniel said with a reluctant grin. Damn Simon, but he could always pull him out of a bad mood.

"You are too kind, my friend," Simon said with a hearty slap to Daniel's back. "Too kind."

* * * * *

Alecia spun around to face Palu as soon as they entered the drawing room. She waited to speak until Nat closed the door. "Are you all right?" He looked wonderful. Big and dark and strong. And so elegant it was hard to reconcile this urbane gentleman with the wild lover she'd come to adore.

He smiled a little sadly. "As well as can be expected." His smile fell. "Thank you for the note."

Nat had been standing silently, but at Palu's words he turned and slammed his fist against the wall. "Damn it!" His anger dissipated as quickly as it had risen. He leaned forward and pressed his forehead to the wall he had just abused. "We should not be here together. It will ruin everything. Everything."

Alecia placed a shaking hand against her roiling stomach. She wanted to touch Palu so much, to jump into his strong arms and kiss his sweet mouth. "Nat, I can't. I just can't. Please, we have to find another way. Surely we can be discreet?"

Palu had paled. "Is it like that, then? You cannot be seen with me?"

Alecia was torn apart at his wounded expression. "No, Palu! Not like that." She reached out to him. "Please, you must let us explain. We don't want to ruin *you.*"

"What?" He was so confused, and Alecia ignored the warning shake of Nat's head.

"It's Hardington," she told Palu, straightening her back and glaring at Nat. "He came to see us."

"Yes, I know." Palu walked over and sat on the sofa, arms braced on his knees and his head hanging.

He looked so dejected that Alecia rushed over and sat next to him, wrapping her arm around him, hugging him. He felt so good, smelled so good, and Alecia grew lightheaded. She'd never thought to have him next to her again.

"Then you know he could ruin you. He could have you removed as a Fellow at the Royal Society." Her voice broke. Nat was right. They had to leave Palu alone. They had to stay away from him, or they would destroy his life, his career.

"What are you talking about?" Palu asked incredulously. He pulled out of Alecia's arms and stared at her aghast.

"Damn it," Nat swore again. He stalked over and threw himself down on the settee opposite them. "We can't risk it, Palu. He swore that as long as we stayed away from you he wouldn't speak to any of the patrons there about our affair." Nat rubbed his hair so roughly it stood straight up on the top of his head. "We won't take the Society away from you," he promised earnestly. "We know how much it means to you."

"This is why you ended our affair?" Palu asked warily.

Nat nodded. "He came to see us not long after you left a week ago." He leaned forward and spoke intently. "You must believe us, Palu. We would never have sought you out. If we had known you were in the park we would never have gone there. We'll explain to Hardington that it was an accident, a coincidence."

Palu smiled wryly and Alecia's heart leapt because there was both humor and a growing lightness in his face, dispelling the dejection of a few moments ago.

"Really?" he drawled. "A coincidence? And how are you going to explain my coming home with you again? We were simply going in the same direction? I'd left my glove in your parlor?"

Alecia bit her lip, not sure whether to laugh at the absurdity of his observation or to cry at the futility of it all. He was right. Hardington would never believe them.

Palu tilted his head in that way of his, the one that said he was trying to understand something. "Why? Why does Hardington want to keep us apart?"

"Revenge," Alecia said softly. Palu turned a surprised look to her. She nodded. "Apparently he has not forgiven you for stealing a lover from him during the war. And when we chose you instead of him at Wilchester's, he set out to punish us all."

Palu laughed in genuine amusement. "Stole a lover during the war? Did he mean William?"

Alecia nodded. "Why didn't you tell us about him?"

Again Palu looked surprised. "It simply never occurred to me," he answered, and it was obvious that he spoke the truth. "William was my lover for several months. We were very close." He looked away and smiled at whatever memory the other man's name had resurrected. "He was my best friend before he was my lover." He shook his head. "He had no interest in Hardington whatsoever." He snorted in disgust. "Hardington was fooling himself if he believed otherwise." Palu rubbed his jaw. "But to give the devil his due, Hardington's pursuit of William is what drove us into each other's arms."

"What happened to him?" Alecia asked, although she thought she knew.

"He died," Palu answered in his straightforward way, "at Albuera." He smiled sadly. "If only he had held out until the rain arrived. The French muskets didn't work when they got wet." He shrugged fatalistically. "Although the French bayonets did."

Alecia placed her hand on his arm tentatively. "I'm sorry."

Palu patted her hand as if offering her comfort. "It happens. We were at war, after all. It was not unexpected."

"Did you love him?" Nat's question was sharp, and when Alecia looked at him he was blushing and frowning. Palu was regarding him intently, his head tilted again.

Palu sighed before answering. "Yes. But...not as you mean, I don't think." Nat just continued to stare at him ferociously and Palu gave him a small smile. "I loved him deeply, as a friend and confidante. But it was always understood that our affair would end when the war did."

Nat visibly relaxed and Alecia realized that he was jealous. She liked to see him that way. It meant his feelings were true.

"That's not all," Nat told him seriously. "Hardington's real motivation is money. He feels that you cost him a great deal of money when you refused to let him invest in your voyages."

Palu surprised them both by laughing. "He's correct," he said with a satisfied grin. "Hardington cannot hurt me," Palu said firmly. "Whatever nonsense he has told you is wrong." He stood and walked over to stand in front of Nat. "The Fellows of the Royal Society do not care what I do in my

110

personal time, Nat," he said quietly. "The patrons only care about the science and the discoveries, and what money can be made from them." He looked over his shoulder at Alecia and then back to Nat. "Are you not a patron?"

Nat shook his head, his face turning even redder than before. He looked over Palu's shoulder, avoiding his eyes. "We do not have the funds to support anyone's research."

"I'm sorry. Of course. But you have been to lectures, and met other patrons?"

Nat nodded hesitantly. "Wilchester is a patron."

"Then you know what I say is correct." Palu sounded so sure.

"But Hardington said that there were several Fellows and patrons who were not happy with your election."

"Yes, but that's true of any Fellow. There are petty jealousies and disputes among us all." He paused and his look became wary. "I am very good at what I do."

"Good?" Nat burst out. "You are the best, and you know it. You are the most celebrated naturalist working with the Society today, not just for your parentage but for your own travels and discoveries."

It was Palu's turn to blush. "Thank you."

Nat threw his hands up in the air. "That means that everyone will be watching you, Palu! There will be talk and all those petty jealousies and disputes will magnify as your detractors try to destroy you."

Palu laughed and Nat glowered. "Nat," Palu said with laughter in his voice, "you think me more important than I am, truly. There are some who will turn away or disparage me and my research because of our relationship, but there are many who do so now simply because of who my mother was."

"What are you saying?" Alecia asked in a trembling voice.

111

Palu looked at her. "I'm saying that if that is your only objection to continuing our affair, then it is easily removed. Hardington has misled you for his own ends."

"Surely you can't want to see us anymore?" Nat asked in anguish. "After what we did?"

Alecia wrapped her arms around her stomach. She'd almost forgotten how they'd betrayed him. It was unforgivable. "I'm so sorry, Palu," she said softly. "Nat is right. We treated you shamefully. It is within your rights to hate us for it."

Palu came and sat next to her, hugging her tightly. She melted in his embrace. He was so strong and warm. She'd been cold to the bone for the last week without his warmth. "Now that is nonsense," he whispered against her hair. "Hate you? I couldn't. Perhaps what you did was wrong, and yes, you hurt me, but I understand why you did it." He gripped her shoulders and looked into her eyes. "I have seen into your hearts, and I know how you see me, and how you treat me. You are not like the others who cannot see who I am past where I came from."

Alecia trembled, almost afraid to believe him. "I've missed you so much," she whispered. She placed her hand on his chest, right over his heart, and felt its furious pounding.

"Then take me," Palu said quietly. He turned to include Nat. "Both of you."

Chapter Nine

୫ର

"No." Palu and Alecia looked at Nat in surprise. He shook his head. "No. If we are going to do this, then we are going to do it right."

Palu gave him a crooked smile. "Well, that was the direction in which I was going."

Nat couldn't hold back an answering grin. But he cleared his throat. "You deserve another explanation."

Palu turned serious at Nat's words. "No, Nat—"

Nat cut him off. "Yes. What we did…it wasn't right, and it wasn't fair to you. But we had our reasons."

Palu stood and walked toward Nat. "We've been through this already. I forgive you," he told him, and Nat knew he meant it. But it wasn't enough.

"Alecia lost a baby several years ago." Palu kept his face as neutral as he could, but Nat could see the pity there. For once he didn't resent it. He looked over at Alecia and she was looking down at her hands in her lap, biting her lip.

"I'm sorry," Palu said, clearly trying to make them both feel better, but not sure how to do it.

Nat smiled sadly. "We were devastated." He took a deep breath then and told Palu what they'd never told another person. "But the baby wasn't mine."

Palu merely tilted his head and waited. Nat truly appreciated the other man's taciturn nature at that point. He would have hated platitudes.

"Alecia stayed true to me for the first two years of our marriage," Nat explained, pacing behind the settee. "She never conceived." He glanced at Palu out of the corner of his eye and saw comprehension in his eyes. "When she began to…entertain other men, after only a few months, she conceived."

"So whatever reason is behind her inability to have a baby lies with you." Palu sounded so cool, as if he was discussing some scientific paper. Nat nodded. "Why did she lose the baby?"

"We don't know," Alecia said. Her voice was strong, but the effect was ruined by a loud sniffle. "After I told Natty about the baby, I thought he'd be so angry. But he wasn't. He wanted a child. He didn't care whose it was."

Nat walked over immediately and sat down next to Alecia. He took her cold hand in his. "It's true, I didn't care. I knew how much Alecia wanted a child, and of course her father is obsessed with it. The baby would have made things so much easier." He cleared his throat again. "And I wanted a child, too. I wanted to be a father."

Alecia gripped his hand tightly. "It just wasn't meant to be." She shook her head as if clearing it and blew out a breath. "After, it brought us closer." She lifted Nat's hand and kissed it and he felt the burn in his eyes, and blinked away his tears. "I didn't want anyone else's baby after that. Only Nat's."

"Ah," Palu said, coming over to sit opposite them. "That is why you don't fuck other men."

Alecia nodded. "Yes. That is why. Because, while we tell everyone I cannot conceive, the truth is I might."

"But if it would make things easier with your father…" Palu let the thought trail off.

Nat glowered at him and wiped his eye with the back of his free hand. "I won't make Alecia do it if she doesn't want to. And I certainly won't have a baby for *him*."

"I understand." Palu's voice was filled with compassion, and Alecia's hand tightened on his again. "I will respect your boundaries, both of you. I will not ask of you anything that you don't wish to give in this relationship. I understand that first there are the two of you."

114

Nat shook his head, appalled that Palu misunderstood so badly. "No, no that isn't what I'm telling you." Now Palu looked confused. Nat wanted to tell him how he felt, but it was too soon. Palu hadn't indicated he wanted more than an affair.

"Alecia and I wish to leave England," Nat said. "We want to have a life somewhere else, far from her father and what is expected of us, and far from our past." He shook his head, not happy with his explanation. "We will have children, and a family, but not here."

"I see," Palu said. "So you are telling me this to make me understand why you tried to use me against Alecia's father."

"Yes." Alecia looked at him beseechingly. "I know it was foolhardy and despicable, but we are desperate. Please do not judge us too harshly."

"When we took you to Colby's..." Nat paused and blew out a pained, embarrassed breath, "I knew it wouldn't work. Unfortunately, I know him too well." He made himself look directly at Palu as he spoke. "I was also trying to distance myself from you." He made a circular motion. "From us and what was happening."

Palu looked at them warily.

"I knew it wouldn't work, as well," Alecia added quietly. "But it seems that every month we come up with some new, equally stupid idea to force the money out of him." She bit her lip, but then straightened her back and licked her lips. "I, too, was afraid of making too much of our brief affair, because I thought that it would drive Nat and me apart again." She turned to look at Nat with such love that his heart swelled in his chest. "I will not lose him again." She looked back at Palu. "But this is what we both want."

"Is it?" Palu asked quietly.

Alecia's silence made Nat turn to look at her. What he found in her face was unsettling.

Alecia wouldn't look at Nat. She kept her gaze focused on Palu. "Is it what I want?" she asked quietly, but in a firm voice that made her proud. "Yes, for the first time in a very long time, yes."

"Alecia?" Nat spoke from beside her, and she could sense his confusion and alarm.

She turned to him. "Oh, Natty, admit it. The men we've brought to our bed have left us both unsatisfied. And I think the main reason for that is...me." She sighed and turned away, biting her lip hard. "I love being with you, Nat, and I love to watch you with other men, but I never truly wanted any of them. When I touched them, or let them touch me, it was all about making you happy."

"Alecia, no," Nat gasped, horrified. "What have I made you do?"

Alecia let out a weak little laugh. "Oh, don't be so melodramatic. I wasn't destroyed by the experiences, by any means." She squeezed his hand. "As I said, I loved watching you with them. And you have always made certain that I found a great deal of pleasure in the encounters. But the pleasure there was in what you and I did together, and had very little to do with whomever happened to be sharing our bed." She licked her lips and felt the blush staining her cheeks, but pushed forward, determined to be open about things at last. "I've never really wanted another man." She turned to look at Palu, thrilled again at his tall, dark, commanding presence, and by her secret knowledge of the inked designs under his fashionable gentleman's attire. She was aroused by the memory of his thick cock, and how he kissed, and what he and Alecia had done to Nat. "Until Palu," she whispered. "For the first time I know what this could be, what we've only played at before." She paused and watched Palu's eyes darken with secret knowledge of her, too. "And I want him. I want us."

She stood and moved away from Nat. She knew that Nat was hesitant to talk of their feelings. So was she. She knew

Palu cared for them. That was his nature. She was sure he wouldn't be here if that weren't the case. But love, and all that love would mean for the three of them? She and Nat had discussed their friends' relationships before and how hard and painful it must be for them to deny one love while acknowledging another. They'd vowed they didn't want it. And now here they were, in love with Palu. She feared rejection, but she also feared causing him more hurt. Yet she didn't want to enter into a full-fledged affair without revealing what she wanted, and to a certain extent, how she felt.

"I fell in love with Nat the first time I saw him." Nat was staring at her, myriad emotions flashing across his expressive, beautiful face. Palu, on the other hand, was watching her with a closed look. How amazing he was with his ability to hide or reveal his feelings in his arresting face at will. "I was only seventeen when we first met. The differences between a seventeen-year-old girl, barely introduced in society, and an eighteen-year-old boy are enormous, by the way." She smiled at the memory. "But Nat was so handsome, and lively, and witty, and oh, so intelligent," she told Palu fervently. He smiled at her, encouraging her to go on.

"I never thought he'd care for me," she said, pulling back the curtain to look out on a late afternoon suddenly warm, with deep purple skies falling into an early sunset. "I was young and stupid and gauche. The only child of an enormously wealthy, indulgent, mannerless merchant thrust upon the upper classes."

"You were never gauche," Nat said dryly, and when Alecia let the curtain drop and turned back to them she was relieved to see Nat had regained his humor and equilibrium. "You knew just how to flirt with a man."

Alecia laughed. "If I did, I didn't know it. Perhaps it was only with you."

Nat's eyes were warm as he smiled. "It would be nice to think so."

Alecia wagged a finger at him. "But don't mislead Palu, Nat. You had no time for me, nor the inclination to make any. You were very much enamored of your string of lovers."

Nat sighed. "Yes, I was. I was the immature one. I married Alecia for her money, and to make my father happy. Have no illusions about me. I found her tolerable, and attractive, and I figured we would rub along well. But I was not in love." He grinned ruefully at Alecia. "I'm sorry, my love."

For some reason his confession of the truth relieved her rather than upset her. She had been there, no amount of lies or rosy recollections could change the past they both knew. "Don't be sorry. That is certainly more than many women get from their spouses." She turned to Palu, loathe to tell him the rest, but determined.

"Nat was right. We had no idea what to do in bed together." She snorted with laughter at some of the memories. "He was completely mystified by the female anatomy, and I the male."

Nat blushed. "I had the basics, I believe."

Alecia bowed her head in acknowledgment. "I stand corrected. You did indeed know where to put what."

Nat suddenly laughed. "That is about all I knew. What a terrible disappointment I must have been to you."

Alecia shook her head. "No, you weren't. I was just so happy that you would visit my bed at all. I had no idea what I was missing."

She looked at Palu. "Nothing to say?"

He shook his head with an amused grin. "No. I'm enjoying the story."

"Hmm," Alecia said as she walked over and sat again, this time next to Palu. He turned to her. "Perhaps you won't enjoy this part." She took a deep breath. "I began to have sexual relations with other men after I caught Nat with one of his paramours, at a party we were attending separately. I went

118

in search of him, and I found him fucking a mutual acquaintance in the library." She turned to a red-faced Nat with a wry look. "He has since refrained from such public assignations." She turned back to Palu and her voice became a little dreamy. "But he was magnificent. The look on his face, his cock so hard, the erotic things he was saying to the man beneath him as he rode him so hard and deep. When he came he threw back his head and he whimpered, and the other man cried out his name as he spent on the Aubusson." She smiled crookedly. "In the middle of his peak, Nat looked over and saw me, but he couldn't stop. And I knew then that I wanted that. I wanted that kind of passion, passion that Nat was clearly reserving for others and not for me."

"Alecia —" Nat began, but she cut him off.

"Uh, uh, uh," she said, ticking her finger back and forth. "It's my turn."

Palu chuckled beside her. "Getting some of your own back?" he teased.

Alecia smiled grimly. "Yes, today and then, too. I walked right out, seduced the first man I came upon in the hallway, and cuckolded my husband in the stables that very night."

Palu took her hand. "Did you find the passion you were seeking?"

Alecia laughed bitterly. "Oh no. I found that men have even less passion for a woman of easy virtue than they do for their wives. I was swived in the hay, and abandoned without so much as a 'thank you' as soon as he came. And as usual, I was left aching." She looked away, ashamed. "And so I tried again, with another man. And then again, and yet again."

Palu squeezed her hand. "And you?" he asked Nat quietly. "How did this make you feel?"

Nat shrugged. "What could I say? I was doing the same. It became almost a joke among my friends, to see who could fuck the most people in the shortest span of time, me or

Alecia." He looked chagrined, and Alecia gave him the smile that said she understood. He returned it.

"And then, Simon?" Palu asked.

Alecia nodded. "Yes. And for the first time I figured out what all the excitement was about." She laughed at the memory. "The first time I came I thought I was dying. It took nearly an hour for Simon to calm me down."

All three of them laughed. "I'm not sure I should laugh," Nat said, amused, "considering that I had never made her come." He shook his head ruefully.

"And you and Simon?" Palu asked him.

Nat nodded. "Yes, well, I'd come before." They laughed again. "But, yes, Simon insisted that I be only with him while we were together, and it was a revelation." He looked at Alecia with hot eyes. "And he liked to talk. He liked to talk about women, which I found rather odd. About what to do to one, how to make them scream and cry and come, and the pleasures to be had when two men took a woman together." He came over and kneeled at Alecia's feet, and he picked up her hand and kissed her palm, and she felt the heat sear all the way from her fingers to her toes, and back up to settle with blazing accuracy in her sex. "And what he described sounded divine. Suddenly all I could think of was Alecia. And that it just so happened I had a woman I thought might enjoy that."

"Did you?" Palu's voice was rough as he asked her the question.

Alecia nodded and closed her eyes, remembering the feel of both Nat and Simon inside her, filling her, fucking her until she screamed. They had never done that with anyone else.

"I never knew you could fuck a woman like a man," Nat whispered. "But Alecia loved it."

Palu's breathing was a little jagged. "I have never done that."

Alecia opened her eyes to see Palu watching her intently. He wanted her so badly she could almost reach out and touch

120

the desire in the air. "You've never had a woman in the bottom before?"

Palu shook his head. "Nor have I ever shared a woman." He blushed a little. "With you and Nat, that was the first time I had ever had two lovers at the same time."

Nat grinned that delicious, wicked grin that said he desperately wanted to do something naughty. "Would you like to?"

"To what?" Palu asked, but she could tell he already knew the answer.

Nat's whispered response made Alecia shiver. "To find out how it feels to fuck a woman with another man? To fill her front and back, and feel me move inside her with you? To truly share Alecia?"

Alecia felt every muscle inside clench in anticipation. *Yes, God yes*, that was what she wanted. When Palu nodded his head, burning a hole through her with his stare, she smiled. "Now you know. *That* is what I want," she whispered.

Chapter Ten

Palu was afraid this was going to be a very short interlude. Just watching Nat and Alecia watch him as he undressed had him perilously close to embarrassing himself. They were so hungry for him. And after listening to them before, he knew their hunger was for more than just the thrill of another man in their bed. They wanted him, and no other. This was about the three of them.

When the last of his clothing hit the floor, Alecia gestured him over to her. She was different today. It was as if she had crossed a border and discovered something new about herself. She'd said that she had never really wanted another man until Palu, had never understood what it could be between two men and a woman. Palu took a step to obey her summons, but then he stopped.

"I never imagined it," he told her.

She stopped in mid-motion, and her hand fell softly into her naked lap as she sat on the edge of the bed. "What do you mean?"

Nat was leaning against the bedpost watching them both avidly, his excitement and anticipation filling the air with a fog of desire. He wanted it, too. He wanted to share Alecia, share the wife he loved, with Palu. And he wanted to share Palu with Alecia, to give her what she'd said she wanted. He, too, it seemed, had crossed some invisible boundary. He was more relaxed tonight, more willing to let Palu and Alecia lead, and he follow.

"I never imagined what it would be like, with a man and a woman."

"Why not?" Nat asked curiously. "You said you'd been with both before."

Palu nodded. "Yes, and I knew people who did engage in those relationships during the war. But I was never tempted. I have always been satisfied with just one lover."

"Then why now?" Alecia asked him. "Why us?"

"Because you are an 'us'," Palu said simply. "Because your love for one another is a part of you, and I want both of you. To have you separately…" He shook his head. "It isn't possible. I can't separate you. Does that make sense?"

Alecia was frowning, a small line appearing between her brows. "So you don't see us separately? As individuals, I mean?"

He blew out a breath. "No, no. This isn't coming out right. I want you, Alecia. I love your golden curls and lush breasts, and your sweet nature. And Nat, I was drawn to him immediately, to his looks, his presence, his laughter. But what I find most appealing is the way you feel about one another, and the fact that, even if it is only for a short while, you are willing to let me be a part of that. I am…" he struggled to find the right word, afraid of saying too much, "attracted to how you love each other."

Alecia looked astounded by his answer, but his words had enflamed Nat. The other man was smiling, but his look was intense and his body was more aroused.

"Most men do not like it," Alecia murmured. "They want to be the focus of our desire and are unhappy when our encounters are more about Nat and me than about them."

"But our time with Palu hasn't been like that, Lee," Nat said softly. He straightened and stood there with his hands hanging at his sides, as if he were displaying himself for Palu's approval. Didn't he know how very much Palu approved already? Hadn't he made that clear? "It has always been about Palu and us, and what we have found together. There is more here than ever before."

Palu's heart was thundering in his chest. They were waiting, leaving it up to him. He took a step toward them, and it seemed larger and more important than it should have. It was merely an affair, wasn't it? What they had found here was wondrous, but it was just desire. Even as he tried to talk himself into believing it, Palu felt that small seed of hope he carried inside burst its coat and thoughts of what could be between them wrapped themselves around his heart like vines.

He chose not to answer, not to speak at all. Instead he took another step and another. He pulled Alecia from the bed and down in front of him as he dropped to his knees before Nat. Nat reached out and ran his hand through Palu's hair, and Alecia wrapped her arms and legs around him, rubbing her breasts against his chest. Palu reached up and gently wrapped his fist around Nat's hard cock and tugged. Nat took the small step needed for Palu to lean just a little forward and take Nat's cock in his mouth.

"Palu," Nat cried out, his hips jerking. His hand clenched in Palu's hair tightly, and it felt so good that Palu groaned. Nat tasted so delicious, hot and earthy and salty. Palu ate at him, sucking and licking and swallowing the moisture leaking from the tip. He wanted this, wanted Nat in his mouth, wanted to taste him, devour him, own a small part of him forever.

"Yes," Alecia whispered, her head on Palu's shoulder. She rubbed against him again, this time not just breast to breast, but also groin to groin. Her sex was wet, the hair a damp tickle against Palu's needy cock.

Palu did not do this for casual lovers. He had done it with William. And he would do it, he desperately needed to do it, with Nat. His cock was just the right size, full and long, but not too long to fit entirely in Palu's mouth. He held Nat's cock there, deep in his mouth, almost in his throat, his nose buried in Nat's pubic hair, and he inhaled deeply through his nose. He could smell Nat, the soapy, musky scent of him, and taste him, a flavor so unique he could compare it to nothing. Palu groaned and he felt Nat shudder as the sound escaped around his cock. Nat tried to pull back, but Palu reached a hand between his legs and covered Nat's sweet arse with it. His hand was so big he could palm nearly all of Nat's muscular cheeks. He squeezed, driving Nat into his mouth deeper.

"Palu," Nat whimpered and Palu growled his approval of that sound. Just then Alecia bit his shoulder, her legs tightening around him. Palu held her closer, crushing her breasts against him and he began to fuck Nat with his mouth.

Nat and Alecia seemed to know what he needed. Nat kept that fist in his hair and fucked Palu, letting Palu set the pace and the intensity of it. And Alecia slid her arms under Palu's and clutched his back while she kissed and licked the *tatau* on his shoulder and chest. It felt so good to have them both enjoying him like this. Sharing him, using him, whatever term applied, Palu cared not. He only cared that they not stop until he was full of them, and they of him.

A constant hum of arousal was escaping from Nat as his tempo increased and his thrusts grew harder. Palu could tell that Nat had no intention of stopping. He did know. He knew exactly what Palu wanted – to taste him, swallow him, own him for a brief moment in time. Alecia shared their excitement. Her breathing was choppy, her heartbeat a thundering wave crashing against his chest. She held him so tightly he thought she might crawl right inside of him, right there next to his heart. She whispered encouragement in his ear.

"Yes, Palu, darling, make him come, make him fill you up. I want to drink him from you, Palu, to breathe you both in. You're so beautiful," she sighed dreamily, "so beautiful."

He reached down and gripped her plump bottom at the same time he squeezed Nat's again. Both of them were his right now, his tonight. He held them and enjoyed them as if he had claim to them.

Nat's whimper turned to a groan, and then he was coming, pulling Palu's hair as he thrust deep into his mouth and filled it with his hot, salty release. Palu drank it like the finest wine, loving the tremors that racked Nat as he spurted over and over until he finally fell back a step with a gasp, pulling his cock from Palu's mouth.

Before he could say a word Alecia kissed him. She thrust her tongue into his mouth and licked deep, a delighted hum vibrating along Palu's tongue as she devoured him. Nat's hand fell to his shoulder and squeezed and Palu gave himself to the kiss. He let Alecia have it all, all that he had and all that Nat had given him. She was practically climbing up his chest before she broke away with a throaty laugh.

"God, you taste so good, Palu," she said breathlessly. "Like Nat and you, and desire and heat and everything marvelous."

Palu laughed, surprised to find himself as breathless as Alecia. He wanted them both so much. He wanted it all, every bit of them. He wanted to shove his cock in their mouths, and fuck Alecia's hot little cunt and Nat's tight arse and, oh God, Alecia's plump delicious bottom. He continued to laugh at himself. He didn't have enough cocks to go around, to do all that he wanted. What to do, what to do?

Nat hunkered down next to him and Alecia with a smile on his face as he watched Palu. "What is so amusing?" he asked lightly.

"Me," Palu told him, his laughter subsiding at the grin on Nat's face, the grin that had captivated him from that first night. "I was thinking I don't have enough cocks to do all that I want to do to you two right now."

Nat laughed and Palu's pleasure at making him do so was almost as great as the pleasure he found in fucking them. Alecia purred and rubbed against him like a cat and he shivered at the feel of her soft, white skin against his, her delicate bones and precious weight entrusted to his care. "Thank God there are enough cocks in this room to do what *I* want to do," Alecia murmured, earning another peal of laughter from Nat and a shudder of desire from Palu.

Nat leaned down with the smile still on his face and kissed Alecia. It wasn't a perfunctory kiss. It was hot and ravenous, almost violent. Palu saw Nat nip at her bottom lip and Alecia moaned, opening up to him. Their tongues tangled in the air, suspended there between them, and Palu didn't think, he just reacted instinctively. He reached out and touched the tip of his tongue to theirs. Nat sucked in a breath and Alecia moaned and both turned their attention to Palu. They licked at his tongue and kissed his lips, and Nat nibbled along Palu's jaw. But it was when they kissed him together, both of them dipping their tongues into Palu's open mouth that he groaned and trembled.

Nat pulled away and Alecia sucked Palu's bottom lip as she retreated until she released it with an audible pop, making Nat chuckle. The sound chased down Palu's back with a breathtaking tingle. "Now," he rumbled. "I need to fuck now."

Nat slid behind him, pressing his chest to Palu's back and he wrapped his arms around both him and Alecia, who was still perched in his lap. Nat licked the rim of his ear and Palu's shaking increased. "Yes, lover," Nat whispered hotly. "You shall take her first, in that luscious bottom, and then I will fill her cunt. And then together we will all fly to paradise."

"Yes, yes, yes," Alecia chanted desperately in a low voice. Her nails dug into Palu's back.

"I want to watch that *tataued* cock fuck my wife," Nat whispered. "I want to see that black ink slip between her plump white cheeks. Will you do that for me, Palu?"

"Yes," he croaked, nearly driven over the edge by Nat's words.

"Good," Nat crooned softly, kissing Palu's temple. "Good."

"Good hardly describes it," Alecia said wryly, and Nat huffed a laugh against the skin beneath his lips. It was the last straw. Palu stood, Alecia in his arms. He walked over and dumped her unceremoniously on the bed, earning a squeal from her, and turned to see Nat still kneeling on the floor, his hands on his knees as he regarded Palu intently.

"Now," Palu said firmly and Nat smirked. But he slowly came to his feet, obeying the subtle command.

"Now," Nat agreed, and Palu's heart skipped a beat.

Nat slid his fingers into Alecia beside Palu's. She gasped and wiggled her hips on the pillows they had stuffed under her.

"Natty," she moaned. "It's enough, I can do it. Please."

"She's so tight," Palu whispered. "Are you sure, Nat?"

He sounded so worried, but at the same time so aroused, so excited by the prospect of what they were going to do. Nat was extremely grateful Palu had sucked him earlier, or he'd be ready to come again right now just from listening to Palu and Alecia. Palu had been making these extremely erotic little growling noises in the back of his throat ever since he and Nat had begun playing with Alecia's tight little arse. Nat didn't even think Palu was aware of the sounds, which made them even more exciting.

"Yes," Alecia mock growled, and Nat almost laughed at the similarities between her and Palu. "Yes, *she* is sure," she said firmly. The effect was lost as Nat twisted his fingers around Palu's inside her and Alecia gave a little shriek of surprise that collapsed into a sob of pleasure.

Nat did laugh at her response, but the sound was dark and hot and satisfied. Christ, he loved when he made Alecia lose control like this. It had never happened with another man, only with Nat. But her barriers were down around Palu. She trusted him. Hell, she loved him. She'd told Nat so. And Nat was ferociously happy about it. Because the freeness in her tonight was different—it was a little wild, a little aggressive. Palu had changed her. Palu had changed him, too.

At the thought Nat leaned over and kissed Palu's shoulder, tracing one of those gorgeous black ink swirls with his tongue. It had become his favorite pastime, to make love to Palu's *tatau*. "Yes," he murmured, his mouth busy tasting Palu's salty, dark skin, "she knows how to take a man here, Palu. She loves it."

"Do you love it?" Palu asked thickly, tilting his head to the side and Nat's mouth traveled up his neck from his shoulder.

"Mmm," Nat said, "yes." He pulled back and looked at Palu from under his lashes. "I love to fuck Alecia in the arse, just as I love to fuck a man there." He shrugged suggestively. "It's so much tighter and hotter, Palu. So deliciously wicked, as Alecia says. Don't you think so?"

Nat could see the memory of the nights they'd spent together slipping through Palu's eyes, leaving them burning with black fire. "Yes," Palu growled. "I loved fucking yours, Nat. And now," he turned and looked down, "Alecia's."

"Then do it, for the last time, do it," Alecia moaned. "Quit talking about it, you two, and fuck me."

Palu laughed and Nat grinned. "Oh, pretty little Alecia, so eager to take my cock in this tight little hole," Palu rumbled, fucking his finger in and out around Nat's. Alecia groaned in desperation and Palu got a wicked little half smile on his face. Nat's cock twitched and leaked and he hoped like hell that Palu was ready, because Nat didn't think he could wait one more minute.

When Palu looked at him, his eyes a little glazed, Nat knew it was definitely time. He eased his fingers out and Palu followed. Without a word Nat poured oil into his palm and waved the bottle at Palu's hand. He filled Palu's hand as well, set the bottle down and the two of them wrapped their fists around Palu's thick cock.

"Christ," Palu said with a shudder, sweat dripping down his temple to get lost in his hair as he tipped his head back and closed his eyes.

Nat would never get tired of this. The realization was a bit of a shock. He'd always enjoyed sexual pleasures. Perhaps more than your average man, even, which was saying a lot. But it had been over a year since he and Alecia had taken another man into their bed, and Nat was ready to admit it was because he had grown tired of it. He'd grown tired of the emotionless, meaningless encounters. But the pleasure he found with Alecia and Palu was something else. It was more than sexual.

He focused on his hand wrapped around the heat of Palu's hard flesh, the inky *tatau* gleaming with oil in the fading light. Nat's hand looked pale next to Palu's dark skin, saved from being delicate by Nat's wide knuckles and thick fingers. He had calluses on his hands from riding, and Palu seemed to enjoy the roughness of them on the velvet soft skin of his cock.

Alecia had pushed up and leaned back on her hands, watching them. "It's just like the first time he fucked you, Nat," she whispered, her eyes riveted on their hands on Palu's cock. "When Palu and I did that."

Perhaps Nat was deliberating trying to recreate that. He wasn't sure. He knew it wasn't necessary. He knew that this first time for Palu and Alecia would be as special as his first time with Palu had been. It would be different, though, because Nat would share this fuck in a way Alecia had not. Nat would actually feel Palu inside her, against him. It seemed a lifetime ago he and Alecia had done that with Simon. He vaguely remembered a sense of excitement, a sense of the forbidden. But tonight there was no sense of committing a forbidden wrong accompanying the excitement coursing through his veins. Instead it felt so very right.

Nat's hand closed tight over Palu at the thought, and Palu groaned and thrust against him. "Nat," he growled. He shoved Nat's hand away. "Enough. I want to come in Alecia, not on her."

Nat laughed self-consciously. "Sorry." He blew out a breath. "I was just thinking how good this all is."

"Alecia," Palu said roughly, staring at Nat, "roll over."

"Gladly," Alecia said fervently. She scrambled over and up to her knees and threw the pillows there to the floor. "Nat, get beneath me," she demanded.

Nat raised an eyebrow as he looked between the two of them. "Oh? Are you two taking over now?"

Palu wrapped his big, slick hand around the back of Nat's neck and pulled him close. "I wasn't aware you were supposed to be in charge here," he murmured against Nat's lips. Then he kissed him. Nat gave up without a fight. Palu's kisses did that to him. He tasted so rich and dark and decadent, and Nat wanted to fuck Alecia with him more than he wanted to breathe.

Alecia grabbed Nat's hand and pressed it to her breast and Nat could feel how fast and uneven her breathing was, and her heartbeat was racing. Alecia rubbed his hand around her breast and then pushed it down to her stomach. Nat broke away from Palu's kiss, reeling, to see what she was doing.

"Rub this all over me," she panted. She reached back and grabbed Palu's free hand and began to rub it on her as well. "I want to be slick with it. I want to slip and slide against your bodies as you slip and slide inside me."

For some reason her request ignited both men. The thought of Alecia covered in oil, glistening and slick all over while they fucked her appealed to Nat in a primal way, and from Palu's growl Nat could tell he felt the same. They rubbed Alecia with their hands, not too rough but not gentle either. Nat kneaded her breasts firmly, coating them with oil. As he squeezed the pale globes of her breasts he leaned down and took one of her nipples in his mouth, licking and sucking on the turgid tip, rubbing and squeezing the plump, firm mound. Palu had moved to her other side and was rubbing his hands over her stomach and the cheeks of her bottom. Alecia writhed between them. Nat had never seen her so wild. When Palu's hand and mouth joined Nat's on her breasts, Alecia let out a strangled cry and jerked in their arms. As one they moved closer to her, boxing her in, and their hands continued to roam freely while they feasted on her breasts.

Alecia wrapped her hand around Nat's biceps and her hips jerked when his hand slid between her legs. Suddenly she wriggled, opening her legs wider and Nat felt Palu's hand glide down to join his. Both men pressed their fingers into her hot, clenching cunt, and before Nat could do it Palu's thumb moved to Alecia's clitoris and began to circle there.

In just a few strokes she came apart in their arms. Crying their names out she convulsed between them, her inner walls vibrating with pleasure. Palu grunted as she came and Nat felt him curl his finger and rub softly inside her. She cried out again and shuddered for a minute more.

"Now you're ready," Palu said in a low, thick voice. "Now this pretty cunt is wet and ready."

"I'm ready for you, too, Palu," Alecia told him breathlessly. "I ache for both of you."

Nat could take no more. He pulled away and lay down on his back and then pulled Alecia so she straddled him. Palu helped her because she was still unsteady from her release. Nat wanted to fuck her now. Now while she was soft and wet and still thrumming inside. She was ripe for them. He pulled her down so that her arse was in the air and her face was pressed to his shoulder.

Palu didn't need to be told. He moved behind her and grabbed her hips and without a word pressed inside her tight passage. He was moving slowly, but Nat felt Alecia tense and a whimper escaped. He could tell by the sound she was biting her lip.

"Alecia?" Palu asked quietly. He was shaking. Nat could see his arms tremble as he held onto her hips. So much control. So much fear for her.

"Please, Palu," she groaned, "please, all of it."

Palu moved and he groaned long and low as he slid further inside. Nat watched that thick cock disappear between her beautiful pale cheeks and it was as exciting and arousing as he'd known it would be. Watching Palu's cock with its *tatau,* his hips and legs and stomach dark with the beautiful, primitive designs as he fucked their Alecia was amazing and astounding and exhilarating. Nat wanted to be in there, too, sharing the moment with them, the physicality and sheer power of that entry.

"Oh God," Alecia cried out, "oh God, Palu," and Nat's own buttocks clenched in remembrance.

"I know, Lee," he said raggedly, rubbing his cheek in her hair, "I know. He feels so good."

"Yes," she sobbed, "it is so good." She sniffed and moaned and rubbed her forehead on Nat's shoulder. "It feels so good to have him inside me at last."

Nat understood what she was really saying. She loved him. She'd needed to have him, to make him a part of her. Nat hoped to God he could do the same before Palu left again. But sharing Alecia was as important. Palu was right, there was an "us" for him and Alecia that was inviolate, inseparable. He loved her so much she was part of who he was. But with Palu, they were different, they were more. In giving to Palu, they gave to one another, in sharing him they came together. Why was it him? Why did it matter? This was the first time they would truly be together, all three of them. But not the last, Nat vowed. They would share each other in every way possible before they had to let him go.

When Nat pushed inside, Alecia thought she'd be torn in two for a moment until the pain passed and then there was only pleasure, mind-numbing pleasure that stole her ability to think, and threatened to take her voice as well. Palu held her tightly under the arms as he slowly lowered her onto Nat's cock. She felt every inch as it entered her. She was tighter than she could ever remember being. Palu's cock in her behind made her that way, and Nat had to work his way inside while Alecia forced her muscles to relax and take him. She could hear her whimpers and cries, but she couldn't control them. She had to trust her two men, because for her there was nothing but the pleasure, no control and no fear.

"Lee, Lee," Nat chanted softly, his voice strained and desperate. His neck arched for a moment, but he jerked his head back down to watch her take him, as if he didn't want to miss a moment of the sight. His face was flushed, his cheeks sharp and his eyes diamond bright. She loved it, she loved him. He wanted this as much as she did. He wanted to see and feel her take both of them, him and Palu. Palu. She felt him behind her, filling her, holding her. He was so gentle and big and warm, his strength and power contained for her, now a part of her. Alecia reached down blindly and gripped Nat's hand where it held tight to her hip, then she reached up and behind, wrapping her arm around Palu's shoulders, and he hunched down so she could reach him, his mouth resting on her shoulder, kissing her, crooning softly to her, caring for her, feeling *her*, Alecia, and no other woman.

When Nat was all the way inside her Alecia could hardly catch her breath. She felt as if she stood on a precipice. Palu gently nudged her forward and Nat hooked his hands under her arms and held her as she came down over him until her breasts pressed into his chest. Her skin felt stretched tight everywhere, so sensitive she felt the air moving through the room, each individual hair on Nat's chest caressing her. Then Palu came down behind her, his hands coming to rest beside Nat's shoulders on the bed. She was surrounded by them, full of them, she breathed with them, their hearts thundered in rhythm, and suddenly she knew. This was joy. This overwhelming love and happiness and anticipation she felt was true, unfettered joy.

She bit her lip but she couldn't stop the tears from filling her eyes. She'd never felt this way. It was magical, wondrous. "I love you," she said hoarsely. She knew Palu didn't understand. But Nat cupped her cheek and made her look at

134

him, and she knew he saw and understood everything. "Love me," she whispered.

"I do," Nat told her and kissed her softly on the lips. "I do."

Alecia shook her head. She needed Palu to know what she wanted. Nat looked worried, but he didn't stop her. "Palu, love me," she asked, waiting, hoping.

He didn't answer. Instead, he began to move.

Palu slid out of Alecia just a mere few inches but that small movement within her tight passage was enough to make him clench his teeth and every muscle he had to hold back his release. He could feel Nat inside her. It was the most incredible thing he'd ever known. To feel both of them so intimately, to know that each move, each breath, each heartbeat was shared by all three. When they had been together a week ago they had shared each others' bodies with hands and mouths and words. But this, this was so much more.

"Palu," Alecia cried out. Her voice was shaking and breathless and it soaked into his skin and heated his blood. She wanted him. She needed him. He leaned down and licked her shoulder and felt her shiver.

"Is it all right?" he whispered.

Alecia laughed weakly. "Yes, yes, better. Perfect."

He pushed back in and Nat whimpered. Palu loved that sound. Loved that he was making both of them cry out with pleasure when he fucked them. He needed to hear them, to push them, to make them feel this way over and over. For a moment he thought about what he'd seen when he'd watched Nat and Alecia fuck that first night, the intensity and need. As he pushed back inside Alecia, driving his cock along Nat's length inside of her he looked down at Nat and with shock he realized that both Nat and Alecia looked at him with the same intensity and need. He hadn't seen it, hadn't wanted to see it, before. There was desire, but there was also tenderness and vulnerability in Nat's face. Palu took that trust and tenderness and gave it back in the rocking of his hips, in the rhythm of his thrusts. He was ready now, ready to see it.

Palu understood at last what he could give them, why he was here. They did love each other, but those early years of their marriage created a chasm they simply couldn't cross. A week ago Nat had told him they wanted to get away, not only from her father but from their past. They wanted a new beginning. Could he give them that? God, how he wanted to be with them for a new beginning.

Right now he could give them what they both craved, the satisfaction of sharing each other. With their other lovers Palu believed that the satisfaction came from returning to one another when the interlude was over. The end of each affair was another chance for the two of them to prove their love. If that was what they needed from him, he would gladly give it to them.

But he thought there was more here with him. Why, he didn't know. But they had told him that they were doing things with him they hadn't done with other lovers. What did that mean? He hoped it meant they were experiencing the same terrifying feelings he was. Alecia had asked him to love her. Good God, couldn't she tell how much he loved her?

The thought brought everything in him to a halt—thought, feeling, breath, heartbeat. He loved her. He loved Nat. He was thirty-six years old and he'd never been in love. He'd never put himself at risk like that. Yet now here he was in love with two much younger, already married people. A man and a woman who loved each other so much they forgave the sins of the past and sought a new, brighter future together. Who did he think he was, interfering in that? Could he love them? He could give them his body as they liked, and secretly, silently, give them his soul. Or he could bare that soul and see what they might discover together.

Alecia shuddered beneath him. He felt every tremor in her warm, sweat-dampened skin, felt the muscles in her back and buttocks flex as she tried to arch into him.

"Love me, Palu," she said again in a broken voice. Nat was staring at him intently, his eyes narrow and bright. Palu couldn't deny it. He no longer wanted to.

"Yes, Alecia," he whispered, lowering himself down onto his forearms, pressing deep inside her, pressing against Nat inside her. They both gasped and he felt Nat's cock jerk as Alecia bowed her back and pushed against him, holding him there. "Yes, I love you," he whispered, his heart beating a terrified tattoo in his chest.

"Palu," Nat groaned. His neck arched as Palu pulled out and slid back in. Alecia's flushed cheek lay on Nat's shoulder and she looked at Palu out of tear-filled eyes. She was biting her lip, and Palu reached out with his thumb and gently pulled it free.

"Tell me," Palu begged. "Don't be silent."

"I love you," she whispered brokenly. "I think I have from that first night."

Palu felt as if a crushing weight was lifting from his chest. He looked at Nat. Were those tears on his temples? Palu reached up a shaking hand and brushed his soft brown hair there and found it wet.

"You know how I feel," Nat whispered. "You know." Nat licked his lips, and Palu wanted to kiss him again. He wanted to make Nat forget he was supposed to be in charge. "Love me, Palu," Nat whispered, and Palu's smile was filled with joy.

It was as if the words freed them all. Suddenly they couldn't fuck fast enough or hard enough. Palu had never known this kind of need. He had to show them how he felt, had to fill them with his cock, his seed, his love. Somewhere in the back of his mind he realized that Nat was trying to set a rhythm. Each time Palu pulled out Nat pushed in. Their cock heads slid against each other and down the shaft as Alecia squeezed them tight, little tremors in her cunt and her arse making both men groan.

Alecia was crying out, but she bucked in their arms, taking them and giving back as they fucked her wildly. Palu pulled back up onto his knees and he wrapped his arm around Alecia's waist and brought her with him. As she rose up it changed the angle for all of them, forcing Nat deeper, and Palu's cock drove more directly into Nat's each time he thrust.

"Yes," Nat hissed. "Fuck me, Palu. Fuck me like that."

Alecia laughed wildly. "No, fuck *me* like that," she said.

He couldn't reply. He was lost, lost. He hadn't known it would be like this. He hadn't known it could be. He tried to focus, tried to grab this moment and make it a memory. The lavender scent of Alecia's hair, the feel of her skin, slick with almond oil and sweat, the heat and pressure of her arse, the first woman he'd ever fucked like this. Palu slid his hand up her arm and buried it in her golden blonde curls, closing his fist until she moaned and leaned back into him.

And Nat. Nat was driving his hips up, his hands gripping Alecia's hips to hold her steady against their driving thrusts. His chin rested on his chest as he tried to hold his head up to watch what they were doing. His shoulders were knotted with effort, the freckles there almost lost in the rosy flush of arousal that painted his pale skin. The muscles in his arms stood out in stark relief and Palu felt an overwhelming urge to sink his teeth into those firm muscles. He wanted to devour him. He could still taste the flavor of Nat's semen in his mouth, feel the beat of the veins in Nat's cock on his tongue.

As Alecia moaned at the grip of Palu's fist in her hair, Nat's gaze flew up and collided with his. Palu felt the tremors inside Alecia as she neared her peak, heard the desperation in her voice. He could see the sheen of sweat on the bridge of Nat's nose and the dust motes flying through a weak beam of late afternoon sunlight as it cut across the bed, and time seemed to stop. Then Alecia jerked free of Nat's hold and began to fuck them, driving herself up and down, small cries escaping with each downward thrust.

Palu grunted and closed his eyes and held still. He didn't want her to hurt herself. She dragged the hand Palu had around her waist down her stomach and pressed it against her cunt, pushing his finger between her wet, swollen lips. He found the treasure she was seeking there, a hard button of desperate desire, and he circled it roughly, pressing against it on each rotation.

"Palu," she screamed.

"I want to come with you, damn it," he growled, and he forgot about being careful. Instead he rammed his cock in her again and again, chasing his release as she sobbed her pleasure. Nat was fucking her just as hard and she loved it, loved them, and she told them so, over and over. Palu smiled with relief as he felt his balls tighten painfully and a tingle of heated sensation raced down his spine. And then he was coming, coming inside her, in hot wet, aching spurts, filling her.

"Fuck yes," Nat cried out, and his shoulders curled up off the bed as he jerked and Palu felt the heat and vibration of Nat's release in Alecia's cunt. Nat whimpered as he came, and Palu's cock somehow managed to revive enough to give him one last bolt of lightning hot pleasure at the sound.

When it was over he just kneeled there, breathing heavily, holding Alecia up. She was limp, exhausted, lying trustingly in his arms, her head turned and her cheek resting on his chest right over his heart. He looked down and caught a small, sleepy, satisfied smile on her face. Nat wore an almost identical smile. Nat's eyes were closed, his hair was dark with sweat, his hands flung out to his sides as his chest rose and fell rapidly with his heavy breathing. They all sounded as if they'd run a race.

"What do we do now?" Palu asked quietly, amused. The ragged and breathless sound of his voice surprised him.

"Nothing, anything," Nat answered in an equally ragged voice. "Does it matter?"

"Everything," Alecia whispered. She raised both arms over her head and wrapped them around Palu's neck in a languid stretch that forced his softened cock out of her passage. "Oh," she cried out softly, sounding disappointed.

"Everything," Palu agreed fervently. He glanced over her shoulder to see Nat sliding his hands up her splayed thighs in a soft caress.

"Yes," Nat agreed, meeting his eyes. "Everything."

Chapter Eleven

The sun had set. They'd cleaned up and had fallen asleep tangled in each other's arms. When Alecia awoke several hours later it was to find Palu at her back while she was pressed up against Nat's chest, her head tucked under his chin. She had never felt so safe and warm as she did then. Now they were all awake, but the others seemed as reluctant to get out of bed as she was.

Palu was stretched out on his stomach, his legs spread, while Nat investigated his *tatau* yet again. Nat was kneeling between his legs while he ran his hands over Palu's buttocks and thighs, tracing the swirls. Alecia grinned at him. He was like a little boy with a new toy. Although she had to admit that she was just as fascinated with Palu's *tatau*.

Alecia half-reclined on some pillows facing them. "I have read," she ventured tentatively, "that women in the Pacific islands have these markings as well."

Palu opened his eyes and smiled sleepily at her. His cheek was resting on the back of his hand. He looked incredibly young and happy in the candlelight. "Hmm, have you?" he answered. "I thought you were unfamiliar with them."

Alecia blushed. "In the past week I have read some pamphlets."

Nat snorted and leaned down to rub his nose in the small of Palu's back. Palu shivered. "And a book or two or three," Nat told Palu. "Don't let her fool you, Palu. She is a voracious reader."

Palu's smile grew. "I can see I shall have to study each night to keep up with her."

Was he teasing? Alecia thought he must be. She would never know as much as Palu. He had traveled the world and had written one of the books she'd read. She didn't realize she was frowning until Nat reached over and smoothed the furrow between her eyes with his finger.

"Don't frown so, Alecia," he chided gently. "Palu was teasing. He didn't mean anything by it."

Palu rolled over to his side, nearly toppling Nat. Nat steadied himself and then settled back down on Palu's thigh. Palu bent his arm and rested his cheek in his palm as he studied Alecia silently. She wanted to squirm under his scrutiny, but she held still.

"I do not question your intelligence, Alecia," he finally said. He picked up her hand and kissed her fingertips. "Why do you?"

Alecia shrugged helplessly. "I was not educated as you and Nat were, Palu," she told him, irritated at his lack of understanding. "I am sure that I shall never know what you two do, no matter how many books I read."

Palu merely grunted and continued to regard her intently for a minute. "Tell me what you learned of the *tatau*," he asked suddenly. Without warning he rolled again, this time to his back, and Nat cried out with a disgruntled, "Stop!" as he nearly fell off the side of the bed. Palu grinned playfully and grabbed Nat's hands to pull him back up onto Palu's legs. The new position made Nat lick his lips as he reached down and began to trace the *tatau* on Palu's stomach and hips, avoiding his groin. When Palu thrust his hips up, trying to force Nat's hand onto his hardening cock, it was Nat's turn to grin wickedly.

"You're not answering me," Palu said, turning to look at her again. "What did you learn?"

Alecia was nervous, afraid to show her ignorance. But inside she knew that Palu would not disparage her. He would answer her questions. And she had so many questions. She leaned over and traced one of the swirls on his shoulder. "Your father's book said that these swirls represent the leaves of the fern. Are there so very many of them there, then?"

Palu nodded as he looked down at her finger where it traced the design. "Yes. They eat them, build with them. They use them in countless ways. The fern is very important to many groups there."

Alecia found that fascinating. "And they grow wild?"

Palu laughed. "Oh yes. It is hot there, Alecia, and humid. Like the orangeries here. Ferns grow everywhere. I myself have catalogued over thirty species."

Alecia blushed again. She'd known that about the climate. "What about the other designs? The dots and the band on your arm?"

It was Palu's turn to blush. "I'm afraid I was in a great deal of pain at the time. My grandfather," he paused and looked up at her, "my mother's father, of course, chose the designs for me. There was a religious ceremony as they applied the *tatau*, and the women sang of its meaning. But I was out of my head and only understood one word of every five." He shook his head. "In some way it identifies me. Other Polynesians would know by looking at them where I was from and who my family is." Alecia was tracing the band around his arm. "That signifies strength. Although what kind I'm not sure."

"Inner strength," she said without thinking. She darted a glance at Palu, who looked surprised.

"Why would you say that?" he asked.

She shrugged. "I think that it must take a great deal of inner strength to grow up as you did, a child of two worlds, one of the first of your kind, torn between customs and loyalties."

Palu reached out and traced her cheek with his knuckle tenderly. "You have understanding, Alecia, which cannot be gained from books."

She bit her lip, not sure what to say but terribly pleased at the compliment. Palu touched her lip and she immediately let it go.

"Many Polynesian women have *tatau* around their mouth," Palu told her.

"Oh yes, I read about that." Alecia made a face. "I do not think I would like that."

Palu laughed. "Their lips are inked black, and surrounded by designs." He tapped the middle of her chin. "And they often have a design here, which looks like an exotic beard of some sort."

Alecia laughed. "How odd! And the men find this attractive?"

Palu nodded. "Very. Only the wealthiest women from the best families have the *tatau*."

Nat was shaking his head. "Do not even think of coloring those beautiful red lips with black," he warned teasingly. "I shall have to restrain you until the urge passes."

Palu didn't laugh. Very seriously he said, "I would not like to see even one inch of your glorious skin with *tatau*, Lee." He ran the back of his fingers down the front of her neck and along her collarbone. She shivered at the soft touch. "You are beautiful," Palu said reverently. "Pale, porcelain, this skin is magnificent." He ran his knuckle over her nipple and it peaked, turning bright pink. "I love the rosy flush that rises under it when you are excited." He looked up at her with dark, fathomless eyes. "I love your skin. I want to cover it with mine, kiss it, worship it." He pulled her down to him with a hand on her shoulder and he kissed the white curve of her breast. "No, do not mar it, Lee. Not ever."

She ran her hand through his rough curls. "I won't, Palu," she promised quietly. It was an easy promise to make. Where on earth would she get a *tatau* in England? Feeling mischievous she added, "Not where you can see it, anyway."

Palu pulled back and she sat up again. He seemed to have lost his teasing mood, and she was sorry to see it go. She looked at Nat and his face told her he'd noticed it, too. He bent his arm and flexed his muscle. "What about me?" he joked. "Shall I get one just like yours, Palu?"

Alecia's breath caught at the image, and she answered before Palu could. "Yes," she said breathlessly. "Oh, yes, Natty, just like Palu's. Both of you with marvelous *tatau* on your beautiful, broad shoulders." She shivered. "How utterly delicious that would be."

Palu wore a knowing smirk. "I do believe she likes the idea, Nat," he said with amusement. Then he looked at Nat and traced a finger over Nat's shoulder and down his arm. Nat shivered and Alecia saw the hair on his arm rise. "I think I would like it as well," Palu said roughly. "I want to trace them with my tongue, as you do."

Nat looked at him in alarm. "I'm not getting *tatau* on my cock no matter what the two of you desire."

Palu laughed loudly and Alecia grinned. Whatever had momentarily bothered him was forgotten. "No, I do not want anyone else handling that. Only Alecia and myself." He mock glared at Nat. "That goes for your tight little white arse, too."

Alecia's heart was racing. What did he mean? Was he staying? Did he want a long-term affair?

It was Nat's turn to become serious. "Never again, Palu. No one else ever again." When he leaned down to kiss Palu, Palu pulled Alecia down as well, and the three sealed Nat's promise with a hungry kiss.

When the knock came at the door Alecia pulled away with a gasp, but Nat was slower to break Palu's hold on him. He didn't comprehend that it was actually someone at the door and not the pounding of his heart at the promises they seemed to be making.

"Nat," Palu whispered, nibbling on his ear. "There is someone at the door."

"What is it?" Nat finally called out in a jagged voice.

"Mr. Colby is here to see you, sir," Soames said through the door.

What? Nat sat up and shook the fog of desire from his head. "Mr. Colby? What does he want?"

"He didn't say, sir. Just that it was urgent and he appears quite agitated."

"Mother," Alecia gasped, scrambling from the bed. She spun in a circle, clearly searching for clothes, unable to focus in her worry. Nat quickly climbed after her and Palu followed.

"Alecia," Palu said, stopping her with a hand on her arm. She fell into his embrace and he held her tight while Nat grabbed his pants and shoved his feet into them.

"Tell him we'll be right there," Nat called through the door. Soames answered in the affirmative. Once Nat had his pants on he grabbed Alecia's undergarments from the chair where she had discarded them and thrust them at Palu. "Help me."

Between the two of them they got her into her dress. She rushed over to her dressing table and grabbed a brush while Nat pulled on a shirt. He stopped when he saw Palu just standing there. "Why aren't you dressing?" he snapped. "We've got to hurry."

Palu looked shocked. "Nat, I cannot come downstairs with you. What will he think?"

"Oh!" Alecia cried out. She spun around, her brush clutched to her chest. Tears traced down her cheeks. "Oh, Palu, please!" She bit her lip and breathed deeply through her nose, and seemed to settle down a bit. "I understand if you do not wish him to know you are here," she continued in a small voice. "But please don't leave. I need you."

Nat's heart felt as if it were in a vise. This is what he'd dreaded, these choices. Palu couldn't be there for Alecia, and Alecia couldn't have him when she needed him by her side. Was this love? Was this what they wanted?

"He's coming," Nat said grimly. He grabbed Palu's pants from the floor and threw them at him. Palu caught them to his chest with a heated look. "Get dressed and meet us downstairs." When Palu hesitated, Nat added, "The journey begins here." Would Palu remember those words he'd told them just a week ago?

Alecia collapsed on the small bench before her table with a sob. Palu's lips thinned, but he never broke his eye contact with Nat. Finally he nodded. Nat nodded back, a silent agreement made, and went to Alecia.

"Father!" Alecia cried as she rushed into the room. She hadn't been able to wait for Palu to dress. He'd promised to come, and she had to believe him. Nat was right behind her.

Her father came up out of his seat. He held the chair arms tightly, and his face was flushed an angry red.

"Is it Mother?" Alecia asked, desperate for news. "What has happened?"

"You will never be allowed to see your mother again," he told her sharply.

Alecia stopped so suddenly she nearly fell over. "What?" she whispered.

"What are you talking about?" Nat demanded angrily. "What have you done?"

"What have I done?" her father rasped. "More to the point is what you have done." He took a step toward her and she could see he was literally shaking with rage. "Lord Hardington came to see me today to warn me that news of your affair with that savage Anderson is spreading throughout the city."

"What?" Alecia whispered. So soon? Hardington must have seen them in the park today. He must have followed them. What were they going to do?

"No one can prove a bloody thing," Nat growled. "And even if they could it makes no difference. Alecia and I are married. What we do in the privacy of our bedroom is no one's business but our own."

Her father hadn't stopped glaring at her and didn't even spare a glance at Nat. "You have ruined me," he yelled at her. "I gave you everything you ever desired, I bought a damned nobleman's son for you, and this is how you repay me?" He advanced and Alecia retreated until her back was to the wall. "You have embarrassed your mother and me for the last time. You will not be welcome in our home. We will cut you on the street. We will treat you like the whore you are. Do you understand?"

Alecia was trembling, she couldn't help it. She'd never seen her father so angry. He meant it. He meant every word.

"You bloody bastard," Nat shouted, yanking her father away from her. "You come charging in here at this time of night, scaring Alecia out of her wits, to threaten her? Over something that is none of your affair?"

Her father turned on Nat with a snarl. "And you, a Gentleman of the Back Door you are," he accused harshly. "I married her to a sodomite and this is my reward. You dragged her to hell right by your side, and her mother and me right with you."

Alecia gasped and her mouth dropped open at her father's ugly words. She saw him draw back his fist and she hollered out a warning, "Nat!"

Suddenly Palu rushed into the room and he threw out a hand, catching her father's fist in his palm. "Restrain yourself, Mr. Colby," he bit out. He turned to her. "Alecia, close the door."

"Let go of me, you bastard," her father yelled as Alecia slammed the drawing room door closed on the stunned faces of Soames and the footman. She supposed she'd have to get new help tomorrow after this.

Alecia leaned against the door as Palu shoved Mr. Colby away. "Unless you want me to bodily remove you from this house and throw you into the street," Palu said calmly, "you will lower your voice and your fists. Do you understand?"

"Do it," Nat snarled. "He deserves the gutter."

Mr. Colby marched several steps away from Nat then turned and pointed a shaking finger at him. "You will never see another penny, do you hear me? Not even pence from me."

Nat took a threatening step forward. "That is Alecia's money. It was her mother's, and now it's hers. If she'd let me I'd have you in court over it."

"Ha!" Mr. Colby laughed viciously. "At least she's not as stupid as you obviously are," he sneered. "She knows that to do that would mean exposing your tawdry offences, and place your life in jeopardy."

Palu's heart stopped and he couldn't catch his breath. Colby wouldn't expose Nat to prosecution as a sodomite, would he?

"You wouldn't," Alecia cried out. "Father, please!"

"You don't need the money now," he told her. He pointed at Palu. "Not now that you have him."

"What are you talking about?" Nat asked him sharply. "The money is ours."

"It is not yours," Mr. Colby bit out. "And I shall see you never get it. Your bloody savage can take care of you now."

Palu saw the incomprehension on their faces. Not many knew. How had Colby found out?

"Good God," Mr. Colby said in disbelief. "Are you both that ignorant? And here I thought it was for the money. But it's not, is it? It's just some new perversion you've dreamed up between you."

"Palu is not a perversion," Alecia said heatedly. "He is a man. And we love him." Palu's heart lurched at her declaration.

In the midst of all this she still claimed him. She had no idea of where it might lead, but she did it anyway.

Mr. Colby put his hands over his ears and gave a cry of despair. "Don't say such wicked things to me! 'We love him', as if it wasn't unnatural and disgusting."

"Palu," Nat said slowly but distinctly, "what is he talking about?"

"I believe he is referring to the three of us together," Palu replied, evading Nat's real question.

"That is my daughter you are talking about," Colby ground out. "*My daughter.*"

"Something you only seem to remember when it suits you," Palu answered bitingly.

"It is not unnatural—" Alecia began but Nat cut her off.

"Stop," he commanded. He had his hands up, and both Alecia and her father stopped talking. Alecia bit her lip hard, and Palu wanted to tell her not to hurt herself. Nat turned to him. "Exactly how is our 'bloody savage' going to take care of us?"

Palu sighed and walked over and took a seat on the sofa. "Your 'bloody savage' has an income of nearly fifteen thousand pounds a year," he told Nat.

Alecia gaped at him and then stumbled over and fell into the high backed chair near the window. "Fifteen thousand?" she whispered in disbelief.

Nat heaved an angry sigh and ran his hands through his hair roughly, leaving it standing on end. "And when were you going to tell us this?" he demanded.

"Why? Does it matter?" Palu had been afraid of this. He deliberately lived beneath his means and hid his wealth. He hated the way people changed toward him when they found out about it.

"Where does it come from?" Alecia asked in consternation. She was frowning again. "Where on earth did you get that sort of sum?"

"My father brought back a literal treasure trove of one-of-a-kind curiosities from his expeditions forty years ago. He sold them for a fortune. He bought property and invested it. He also wrote several books, all of which are still sought today."

At his explanation Alecia looked dumbfounded and Nat angry and despondent.

Mr. Colby laughed nastily. "Did you hope to buy them? Well, I've made it easier for you, Anderson. They have nothing now, thanks to you. I'm sure they'll be open to an offer."

Yes, that was what he'd been afraid of. One of the many things. But he realized he wasn't worried about that anymore. He knew them better now. He knew they weren't like that.

"Get out," Nat said, his voice low and angry. He walked over and pulled the door open with restrained violence. "Get out, Colby, and don't come back. We don't need your money."

Colby laughed harder. "No, you don't, do you? You have his now." He pointed at Palu. "Perhaps you're not as big a fool as I took you for, Digby. You sought out richer territory, didn't you?"

"I cannot believe you are my father," Alecia said slowly. She stood and shook out her skirts, staring at him with calm dignity. "All my life you have bullied those around you, including me. I am through with it and with you. I do not need you or your money. My husband has asked you to leave. I ask that you not come back. Ever."

Colby snorted and waved a hand dismissively at her. "Do not worry. I will never be seen here again. I have worked too hard to get where I am to let your promiscuity and perversion ruin all that I have achieved." He walked over to the door, glaring at Nat who still stood holding the door open. "You both have been an embarrassment to me for years. My efforts to curtail your lewd and outrageous behavior have failed. Do not apply to me when you reap your just rewards." He went through the door and turned to say something else, but with a look of supreme satisfaction Nat slammed the door in his face. Colby bellowed for his hat and gloves and a minute later they heard the front door slam.

Colby's removal from the house seemed to cut an invisible cord and both Nat and Alecia found seats and slumped in them.

"Well, it's over then," Nat said morosely. He sniffed and turned his head away to stare at the far wall.

Alecia nodded from her chair, and Palu saw her dash a tear away.

"You needn't worry about your father," Palu told her. "He was right. I have the means to support you both. You need have no fear on that account."

Rather than reassure her, his remark made Alecia hiccup as her tears fell faster. Nat's reaction was typical Nat, as Palu was beginning to see. He threw himself from the chair and pushed his hands into his hair again, this time fisting them on top of his head and giving a frustrated, wordless cry. Palu was taken aback.

Nat's arms fell to his side. "Don't you see?" he asked Palu in a tortured voice. "We can't let you. Everyone will think we have deceived you for your money. I have no wish to be known as that sort of man."

It was Palu's turn to be dumbfounded. "What? What are you saying?"

"I'm saying we can't be with you anymore," Nat cried out. He rubbed his hands vigorously over his face and then stood with hands on hips staring at the ceiling for a moment. When he looked back at Palu the anguish written in his face soothed Palu in spite of his words. He didn't want to Palu to leave. That was obvious. And by God, he wasn't going anywhere. Not now. Not ever again. Not without these two.

"Don't be ridiculous." As soon as the words were out Palu knew he'd spoken rashly.

"Ridiculous? I'm being ridiculous because I don't want people to call me names behind my back, to question my feelings for you, to believe that I would let myself and my wife whore ourselves for your money?" Nat's anguish was turning to anger, which was better in Palu's opinion.

"No, you're being ridiculous," Palu told him as he stood and faced him, "to even think that I would let you go now." He included Alecia in his hard stare. "Or that I would let you push me away."

Alecia stood as well, her arms wrapped around her stomach. "Palu, you must. Nat is right. People will think the worst of us. If we have nothing else, at least we have our pride."

Palu sliced his hand through the air, for once letting his anger show. "Pride be damned! What do you think people will say of me?" He jabbed his finger roughly into his chest. "They will say I am a fool to think that two young lovers such as you could care for me. Me, some half-breed native bastard?" He threw his hands in the air. "And yet I don't care! Let them talk. They have been talking about me since I first set my feet on this shore. All I care about is what we have, what we could have. Don't you understand how I feel? Don't you understand what you mean to me?"

Alecia had covered her mouth with her hand and was shaking her head as her tears fell unheeded. Nat was staring at him with hungry, hopeful eyes. "You are not a fool," he said softly.

Palu walked around the sofa and grabbed Nat's hand and dragged him over to Alecia. Then he wrapped them both in his arms tightly. "You have given me a place," he whispered into Alecia's hair while Nat buried his face against his shoulder. "I have wandered and searched for a place to belong, and I have found it in you two. I'd given up hope, you know. I thought I would always be alone. And now I know that I never will be again. That is worth any price."

Alecia clung tightly to him. He could feel her fist clutching a handful of shirt at his back. "Palu," she sobbed. Nat was silent, but Palu felt his trembling.

"Tell me you feel the same," he begged harshly. "Tell me I am not dreaming. Tell me that wherever you are you will let me be there with you. Here, anywhere. I will give you both the world. Take it. Take me."

"I don't want the world," Alecia cried out. She raised her face to him, cupping his cheek in her palm. "I just want you, us, this. Are you sure?"

Palu nodded, too emotional for words. Alecia rose on tiptoe to kiss him passionately, and he returned her fervor. But he held tight to Nat as well. He wasn't letting either of them go. Not for a long while.

He could taste Alecia's tears, and he swore he never would again unless they were tears of joy. Gradually he became aware of Nat's silence, and he pulled slowly away from Alecia. The look of desire and adoration on her face was one he would never forget.

He turned to Nat and with a finger under his chin lifted Nat's head from his shoulder. "Tell me," he demanded softly. "Tell me."

Nat nodded. He'd been too overwhelmed to speak—but no longer. "Yes. I'll take you, Palu. And I will take the world with you." Palu rested his forehead against Nat's. Even that small kiss of skin on skin made Nat's heart race.

"Where is my laughing Englishman?" Palu whispered. Nat smiled weakly and he grinned. "You will have to do better than that." He leaned in and whispered in Nat's ear, "Will you laugh when you are fucking me, pretty Nat? I would like that."

"Christ, Palu," Nat choked out, "I'll be lucky to live through the experience." He closed his eyes and envisioned

Palu's gorgeous buttocks with their dark designs and he shuddered in arousal. "I wanted to fuck that gorgeous arse of yours the first time I saw it."

Palu laughed that deep, rich laugh that made Nat's blood run hot in his veins. "Have you, Natty?" Palu purred. "I have wanted you to just as long." His voice lowered to a growl. "Ever since you couldn't keep your mouth off it."

Alecia laughed and it was relieved and wild and aroused. She broke away from them and collapsed against the back of the sofa, her arms flung over her head in abandon. "And I have wanted to see it just as long," she cried in delight. She looked at them with glowing, smiling eyes, drying her cheeks with her palms. "Are you going to make me wait much longer?"

Palu pulled away from Nat with another laugh. "One minute you are shy and crying and the next you are demanding that your husband fuck me." He smiled wolfishly. "I love that you are like this with us."

Alecia looked affronted. "I am not shy," she protested.

Nat couldn't help it, he laughed with Palu. "Lee, my darling, you are shy. You are also intelligent and passionate. But you are indeed shy."

She crossed her arms over her chest and glared mulishly. "I asked Palu to come home with us the first time, didn't I?"

"I think that had more to do with Simon taking you by surprise," Palu observed dryly. "And I might add he took me by surprise as well. I had not told him how much I wanted you." Palu stalked Alecia, nimbly maneuvering around the table in front of the sofa. Alecia watched him warily. "And when you brought me home, you sat there on that sofa and blushed and had no idea what to say to me, or what to do."

Alecia blushed. "I knew what I wanted to do. I just didn't know if you wanted to do it, too."

Nat burst out laughing. "His hard cock in those tight breeches should have given you some idea, Lee."

"You mean, like this?" Palu asked, looking down at himself. He was hard, his cock outlined by his buckskins beautifully. It made Nat's mouth water, and Alecia stopped blushing, her look turning hungry.

"Tell me what you want me to do," Nat said, purposefully using the same words as he had their first night.

"I want to be naked for you both," Palu said. "And I want you to fuck me."

"Ah God, Palu," Nat groaned. "That's what I want too."

"Then stop talking about it," Alecia told them, exasperated. She stood up and grabbed both their hands, first Palu's and then Nat's, and dragged them over to the drawing room doors. She grasped the handles and looked at them over her shoulder with a mischievous grin. "Ready?"

Nat felt as if she were asking so much more with that one word. Were they ready for the challenges they would face? Ready to finally leave England with Palu and find the life they'd always dreamed of? Ready for love and a family and all that came with those responsibilities?

"Absolutely," he said, and Alecia threw open the doors and pulled them both through.

Epilogue
Five Years Later

ॐ

"Papa!" The little boy ran across the deck and threw himself into Palu's arms, only to be raised high and swung around until he laughed uncontrollably.

"Gordon!" Alecia chastised. "You know you are not to run on deck."

"But Mama," he argued, "how else was I supposed to jump so high into Papa's arms?"

Palu laughed and ruffled his dark brown curly hair. He couldn't believe how much Gordon looked like him. He considered it a blessing, but when they reached England it would be more of a curse, he supposed. They expected to reach London by mid-week, and Palu was getting more and more nervous about it. Nat and Alecia were the calm ones. They simply shrugged and Nat had said philosophically, "What is, is." Palu had no argument for that.

"You are like two peas in a pod," Alecia laughed, echoing his thoughts. She saw the look on his face and wrinkled her nose. "Don't start, Palu. We've been through this. We will all be fine." She turned and frowned out at the horizon. "I'm more concerned about how the Society will react to my paper. It's very frustrating that I can't be there to read it myself."

"Perhaps someday they will allow women, my dear," Nat said from behind them, "and then you shall be able to present your own papers."

Palu turned and had to smile at the picture Nat made with little Grace asleep on his shoulder. Like Gordon, she had Palu's dark, curly hair, but unlike Gordon she had fair skin and Alecia's features. Nat doted on her, as did they all. She was only two, but she ruled the family with an iron fist.

Alecia reached out and patted Nat's arm. "I am sure that you will do a marvelous job reading it for me, Natty," she told him. "And Sophie is going to have the salon where I will be able to answer any questions later." She bit her lip nervously. "It's not the presentation that worries me, but the content. The Royal Society seems to be full of the physical and medical sciences these days. I don't know how interested they're going to be in the family structure and home life of different native groups in Polynesia."

"About as well as they will receive my paper on the reefs of Australia, I suppose," Nat said mildly.

"Well, Nat, you could always show them your *tatau* and describe the process," Palu mused jokingly.

"I thought that was for your and Alecia's eyes only," Nat teased.

"But Papa Nat, I've seen it," Gordon interjected with a frown.

Palu laughed. "Only for family eyes, then, little man," he said, kissing Gordon's temple.

Alecia leaned over and kissed Nat's shoulder gently, careful not to wake Grace. "Yes, just for the family."

"Can we show everyone yours instead, Papa?" Gordon asked eagerly. "You have more."

Palu choked and Nat laughed. "You brought it up," Nat told him with a raised brow.

Palu looked sternly at Gordon. "Papa was only teasing, Gordon. We don't show or talk about our *tatau* to outsiders."

"Not even Mama's?"

Alecia blushed. "*Especially* not Mama's," she said fervently. "Gentlemen do not talk about a woman's legs at all in public, and most certainly not about any *tatau* they may have on them."

"Why not?" Gordon asked. "Don't they know you've got them under your skirts?"

Palu couldn't control his laughter. "Good Lord, do you really think England is ready for this family?"

Alecia smiled beguilingly. "I don't care. This is my family. England can go hang."

"Mama!" Gordon clapped in delight and Alecia kissed him on the cheek.

Palu silently agreed with her. He looked down and saw a large school of dolphins swimming alongside the ship. "Nat, look," he pointed.

"The Americans on board call it a *pod*," Nat told him, looking over the side, careful to keep Grace away from the rail.

"Do they?" Palu asked with a smile. "Perhaps you will have something to study here after all."

"Well," Nat replied, amusement coloring his tone, "we shall see at journey's end, won't we?"

Palu reflected on the changes the last five years had wrought in all of them. "Our journey is far from over," he said quietly. "There is still so much more to discover."

Nat and Alecia looked at him, and he could see the memories in their eyes, the love and contentment on their faces.

"We are the territory to be explored," Alecia murmured.

"Let the journey begin," Nat responded with a smile.

Palu didn't answer. He simply turned his face to the wind with a smile and let the adventure take him.

The End

Also by Samantha Kane

℘

About the Author

℘

Samantha has a Master's Degree in History, and is a full time writer and mother. She lives in North Carolina with her husband and three children.

Samantha welcomes comments from readers. You can find her website and email address on her author bio page at www.ellorascave.com.

Tell Us What You Think

We appreciate hearing reader opinions about our books. You can email us at Comments@EllorasCave.com.

Why an electronic book?

We live in the Information Age — an exciting time in the history of human civilization, in which technology rules supreme and continues to progress in leaps and bounds every minute of every day. For a multitude of reasons, more and more avid literary fans are opting to purchase e-books instead of paper books. The question from those not yet initiated into the world of electronic reading is simply: *Why?*

1. *Price.* An electronic title at Ellora's Cave Publishing and Cerridwen Press runs anywhere from 40% to 75% less than the cover price of the exact same title in paperback format. Why? Basic mathematics and cost. It is less expensive to publish an e-book (no paper and printing, no warehousing and shipping) than it is to publish a paperback, so the savings are passed along to the consumer.

2. *Space.* Running out of room in your house for your books? That is one worry you will never have with electronic books. For a low one-time cost, you can purchase a handheld device specifically designed for e-reading. Many e-readers have large, convenient screens for viewing. Better yet, hundreds of titles can be stored within your new library — on a single microchip. There are a variety of e-readers from different manufacturers. You can also read e-books on your PC or laptop computer. (Please note that Ellora's Cave does not endorse any specific brands.

You can check our websites at www.ellorascave.com or www.cerridwenpress.com for information we make available to new consumers.)

3. *Mobility.*   Because your new e-library consists of only a microchip within a small, easily transportable e-reader, your entire cache of books can be taken with you wherever you go.

4. *Personal Viewing Preferences.*   Are the words you are currently reading too small? Too large? Too... ANNOYING? Paperback books cannot be modified according to personal preferences, but e-books can.

5. *Instant Gratification.*   Is it the middle of the night and all the bookstores near you are closed? Are you tired of waiting days, sometimes weeks, for bookstores to ship the novels you bought? Ellora's Cave Publishing sells instantaneous downloads twenty-four hours a day, seven days a week, every day of the year. Our webstore is never closed. Our e-book delivery system is 100% automated, meaning your order is filled as soon as you pay for it.

Those are a few of the top reasons why electronic books are replacing paperbacks for many avid readers.

As always, Ellora's Cave and Cerridwen Press welcome your questions and comments. We invite you to email us at Comments@ellorascave.com or write to us directly at Ellora's Cave Publishing Inc., 1056 Home Avenue, Akron, OH 44310-3502.

erridwen, the Celtic Goddess of wisdom, was the muse who brought inspiration to story-tellers and those in the creative arts. Cerridwen Press encompasses the best and most innovative stories in all genres of today's fiction. Visit our site and discover the newest titles by talented authors who still get inspired - much like the ancient storytellers did, once upon a time.

Discover for yourself why readers can't get enough of the multiple award-winning publisher

Ellora's Cave.

Whether you prefer e-books or paperbacks,

be sure to visit EC on the web at
www.ellorascave.com

for an erotic reading experience that will leave you breathless.

Made in the USA
Lexington, KY
03 July 2010